THE HEIRS OF THREE OAKS

THE HEIRS OF THREE OAKS

A Novel of the Old West

by

Ardath Mayhar

Writing as "Frank Cannon"

The Borgo Press
An Imprint of Wildside Press

MMVII

SECOND EDITION

CONTENTS

FOREWORD

When I first began writing westerns, I was determined to avoid as many clichés of the genre as I could manage. First of all, I knew that families were extremely important to everyone, no matter what the historical era involved, and writing a western story without taking into consideration the effects of the plots on the families involved was illogical.

Then I knew from family history, as well as a wide reading in journals and other contemporary records that the women who went west were not the wimpy or whorish sorts depicted in all too many novels and movies. I wanted to show real people dealing inventively and bravely with unusual and interesting challenges. In each of these three books I feel that I may, to some extent, have succeeded in reaching some of those goals.

—Ardath Mayhar (Frank Cannon)
Chireno, Texas
2006

CHAPTER ONE

He could see the corner of a WANTED poster flapping in the wind as he rode up to the post office-store that was the main feature of Dry Wells, Texas, population seventy-three. That information had been gleaned from a leaning sign that showed some evidence of having been planted with community pride and hope...some fifty years in the past.

As he hitched Mule Ear to the corner post of the porch, he managed to get a better look at the sign. It was him, all right. The little error of judgment he'd made in East Texas looked as if it might haunt him for the rest of his life. Robert John Willingham was the name under the picture. He smiled beneath his lush blond moustache.

With the beard and the long hair, not to mention several years of travel in the blazing Texas sun, he wasn't uneasy about being recognized. Not very uneasy. Only his bright blue eyes might betray him, and he now had developed a squint that the dapper young man in the picture had never displayed:

He straightened his hat, tucked his shirt more firmly into his faded denims, and started toward the weather-beaten door of the store. Before he could reach it, the panel erupted outward, and a bleating goat came barreling across the porch and headed for the horizon.

It was followed immediately by a small sturdy woman wielding a broom-handle. She was flushed with exercise and anger, in about equal proportions, and she looked as if she might not mind laying into him, just on general principles. Robert backed up a step. "Whoa, lady, I just got here!"

She glared after the fast-disappearing goat. Then she dabbed at a strand of black hair that was flipping into her face in the brisk wind, using the back of her wrist. He could see that her hands were sticky...it looked like molasses.

"Could I help out?" he asked her. "Looks as if you and that goat had more than just a philosophical discussion."

That made her look at him...really look, not just run her gaze past him. A curl of grin moved the corner of her mouth, and then she began to laugh.

"You might say that," she agreed. "Come on in, if you can find a clean spot to step. That damn goat turned over the molasses barrel. It sneaks into the store with customers. It climbs through the back window. It drives me crazy."

"Why don't you shoot it?"

She looked at him, astonished. "I couldn't do that! When he's not being a complete nuisance, that animal's a friend of mine!"

Robert found himself grinning. Once she got herself together a bit, she turned out to be a nice-looking girl. Maybe twenty-five or so. Not the sort he liked personally, of course, being as he preferred clinging women. This one was, he could see at a glance, as independent as a hog on ice.

"You just passing through?" she asked as she moved past him toward a corner in which stood a bucket and a mop.

"Actually, I'm here about a job. Do you know a man named Jebediah Cobb?"

She stopped in her tracks and turned to stare up at him, her black eyes flashing. "Unfortunately I do. What sort of job do you think that side-winder might have for you?"

Robert felt a bit puzzled. From the letter he'd received, via a tortuous route that didn't include any legal mail service, it sounded as if Cobb might be a real big-wig in Dry Wells. A ranch of forty thousand acres and a big cattle operation had to count for something in a scroungy little place like this.

"He didn't exactly say. Just wrote me that he needed a hand. He...knows some folks I know." And that was no lie. What Robert had no intention of telling her was the fact that the mutual acquaintances were the worst sort of owl-hoots imaginable. And the job had to be illegal—why else choose a hand off a wanted poster?

"He's a scoundrel. I can't see any decent man wanting to

work for him," she said. "I don't trust him as far as I can throw —that goat. And we here in town feel as if he's not treating those boys right at all."

"What boys?" Robert felt as if she might talk more than she intended, just because she was still upset about the mess on the floor and was heated up considerably.

"His wife's nephews. Lovely boys. Andrew's thirteen. Crippled, but he's the brightest kid you ever want to see. And Kenneth is seventeen. Almost old enough to begin running his own property now, but I can't see Cobb turning loose the reins for anything." She was mopping furiously, having doused the molasses with soap and water from the bucket.

Robert stepped back to get out of the way of a sticky stream. "Well, all I want is an honest job. I guess they run cattle on the ranch...that's what he said in the letter I got."

"Oh, yes. What's your name, by the way? If you're going to work around here, you'll be getting mail here at my post-office." She gave a vicious swipe beneath the potbellied iron stove.

"Robert Evans, ma'am," he said. He even had papers to prove it, if anybody ever asked. Robert John Willingham had been left behind in the dust of that con-job back in Nacogdo-ches.

"Well, Robert Evans," she said, leaning on her mop-handle and surveying him closely, "you'd better watch your step out there at Three-Oaks. Nasty things seem to happen to people who work there. And even to the people who own the place. The boys' parents were killed when a twister hit the barn they were working in. The aunt, Letitia, came sailing in to run things, and the first thing you know she'd hitched up with Cobb, which was a fate almost as bad as the buggy accident that killed her last year. Old José is ailing, and hands come and go mighty fast."

"A man's got to eat," he observed, as she returned to her battle with the now vanquished molasses. He felt that he would hate to get on the wrong side of this strong-minded woman.

"What's yours?" he asked.

"My what?"

"Your name. I've introduced myself all nice and proper.

Now what ought I to call you besides ma'am?"

A hint of that grin touched her mouth again, but she quelled it. "Minta. Miss Minta Granger, postmaster and proprietor of Dry Wells General Store and Post Office. That satisfy you?"

"Yes Ma'am, Miss Minta. Now might I ask you how to find the Three Oaks Ranch? I appreciate the warning, but caution makes mighty poor eating."

She leaned the mop against the counter and led him onto the porch. "You go out north about four miles," she said, pointing. "The track isn't used so much any more, so it's dim. Still, you can see where the road into Three Oaks turns off...there's three big rocks piled up right there on your left.

"You turn there, though you can't see a sign of anything in particular for another five miles. The land rolls, over in that direction with little stands of oak scrub spotted around. But you'll find the house at the end of that track. And Jebediah Cobb, bad cess to him!"

"Thank you a lot, Miss Minta," he said. "You suppose I might buy a sarsaparilla, while I'm here and all hot and dusty from the road?"

"Out," she said. "Be more on Thursday, if you want to make that long trip back for it."

"Then I'll be on my way." He didn't like the way she was glancing from his face to the poster and back. Surely there wasn't a sign of that slick youngster left in him after four years! But she was a sharp one. He didn't wait around for the penny to drop.

He unhitched Mule-Ear from the post and mounted. As he rode up the track to the north, he felt her gaze fixed on his back. Like an itch he couldn't scratch. He decided that he wouldn't make many trips in to Dry Wells General Store and Post Office, sarsaparilla or no.

The road was dim, little traveled, though it was a main road between the county seat and the railhead. There were few people in the area, he could tell just by looking across the rolling land. From time to time a lanky cow or a buzzard or a hunting hawk came into view, but not a house, not a barn, not a single person did he meet before he found the three stones.

He sat on Mule-Ear, thinking hard, before turning off onto

10

the almost invisible trail across the scanty grass that covered the undulating land. Cobb sounded funny to him. Most big land-owners in such a poverty-stricken country were respected. Or feared. Cobb seemed to inspire nothing but contempt in Minta Granger, at least.

The situation sounded odd, too. He didn't really own all this land. He was managing it for his nephews...no, his wife's nephews, which made them no kin at all and probably nothing but a thorn in his side.

Did he want somebody to kill them for him? If the death of his wife had been intentional, he might have decided to do something before his older nephew got old enough to take over from him legally.

"I am no killer," said Robert aloud to a passing crow. "A con man, yes. A killer, no. But I might as well see what the man has to say before I turn him down."

He clucked to the horse and the sorrel whickered tiredly and plodded along the trail. Robert looked from side to side, ahead and behind, but there was nothing to see. No cattle. No hands. None of the fencing that was turning the range into a jig-saw puzzle.

A mile, at least, went past uninterestingly. The trail curved to miss a knoll, and as he came around the thing a shot cracked, and the slug zinged off a rock ahead of Mule-Ear.

Robert pulled the sorrel to a stop and put his hands con-spicuously into the air.

"Who're you and why're you here?" came a call from the adjoining fold of land.

A horse came into view...a big, nondescript beast that looked able to carry a gorilla. The man astride him was so thin that Robert was sure the animal didn't even feel his weight.

The Winchester was across the saddle, ready for action. The man stopped at some distance and surveyed Robert coolly. His eyes were squinted with long living and working in the sun. His face was weathered to the shade of a good leather saddle, but beneath the tan was a hint of gray—this was a sick man, holding himself a little too stiff in the saddle to keep from giv-ing in to some hidden pain that was eating away at him.

Robert was used to sizing up people in a hurry. As a con-

11

man, it was part of his stock in trade. He knew, partly by intuition, partly through knowledge of men, that this was one of the tough old breed that never sold its honor and would fight past death for what he thought was right.

"Your name José?" he asked. "Mine is Robert Evans. Mr. Cobb wrote me a while back. Wants me to work for him."

The man went even more still and stiff.

"I am José Meléndez," he said. "Cobb has told me that you come. Be warned, however. Any harm that comes to those children of my mistress through you, that I will avenge. Hear my words, I mean them."

Robert knew that. It rang through the tone and the stance of the man.

"*Hombre,* do I look like some hired gun?" asked Robert in a mild tone. "If I do, the breed has changed a lot."

Now José was really looking at him, and Robert knew he was seeing a middle-sized, nondescript fellow who didn't look as if he could even wrangle cattle effectively. He had cultivated that look with all his might and he knew how well it worked.

The man relaxed minimally. "You do not look like a gunman. But that is no assurance that you are not a killer. Remember my words."

"José, I've never killed anybody in my life. And I don't intend to start now." Truth rang in those words, too, and for once they were no con. Robert stuck to his own game and he had no intention of killing a couple of kids in order to enrich their not-quite-uncle.

"I am foreman here," said Meléndez. "If you work, you work for me. Cobb...." he grinned, showing a snaggle of yellowed teeth. "...cannot dismiss me. My mistress's will forbade that, so long as I live. Even when I cannot work, I will live here and watch over her sons. That is what the will said. That is what I will do."

Robert chuckled. "I'll bet your boss just loves that!"

Surprised, the foreman let slip a grim smile. "It is not a thing upon which he looks with satisfaction," he said softly.

"So then can I go on up to the house and see if I'll be going to work for this cheerful gentleman you work for?" asked Robert.

"Over the next ridge. And take care—I will be watching you."

Again, Robert rode away, feeling a gaze needling into his backbone. He had no intention of killing anyone, and now he wondered if it would be safe to take any job at all. If something happened to one of those boys, he had the feeling that José might well shoot first and inquire into the circumstances quite a bit later.

CHAPTER TWO

The house at Three Oaks had been built on the bank of a creek that ran diagonally northwest to southeast. The three oaks were still there, huge trees, not tall but thick-bodied and gnarled with age. The roof was dusty, the walls of dust-colored stone, the bare yard inside the stacked-rock fence also dusty. Only the gray-green of the oaks and the silver-gray of cottonwoods beyond along the creek gave any change of hue.

Robert rode to the wall and dismounted. "Hello, the house!" he called, with polite caution.

He ground-hitched Mule-Ear and pushed open the rickety gate into the yard. He could see that roses still clung stubbornly to the posts of the porch, their blossoms withered with drought, though spots of moisture about the roots showed that someone was trying valiantly to keep the plants alive.

"Anybody home?" he called, though a column of smoke from the chimney at the rear told him that someone was cooking supper. It was too late, he felt sure, for the master of the house to be out on his range.

"Hello. Who're you?" The voice came, unexpectedly, from beneath the high porch, and as Robert stared a small boy came wriggling from beneath the structure and stood, slapping dust from his pants and ragged shirt.

Now that he was erect, the newcomer could see that the boy was not as young as his size would indicate. His left leg was withered, drawn at the knee, and his entire body looked as if it had undergone some terrible accident that left it warped and under-sized.

"I am Robert. You must be Andrew?"

The boy stared up at him intently. "Yes. How did you

know?"

"Miss Minta Granger, at the store, told me about you when I asked directions. She said you were very bright, but that you had an accident." It wasn't exactly, of course, but crippled was not a word he would have applied to this alert creature.

"Yes, I remember Miss Minta. It's been a long time. Is she still pretty?" asked the boy.

Robert, considering the matter, felt that he might truthfully answer yes. "She is. Very pretty, though a bit snappish. She'd just lost her temper with a goat, in fact."

The boy began to laugh. "Winthrop. I hear tales about him, even way out here. The hands tell us all the crazy things he does. Miss Minta loves him, don't let her fool you. Anybody else would have shot him a long time ago."

"I suspected as much," said Robert. "Is your uncle around? I need to talk with him."

The brightness faded from the pale face as if quenched like a candle. Robert could see the pinched, bluish tinge under the cheekbones and at the temples as the child turned toward the house.

"Oh, he's in there. Doing his bookkeeping...with his head under a handkerchief, snoring the house down. Ken tried to talk to him again today about learning the ropes. Getting to know all about the financial situation of the place, how many cattle, the markets...all the things he's going to have to know in just a few more years. Jed Cobb knocked him down the steps and kicked him while he was out."

Robert winced at the raw hatred in the boy's voice. More and more this looked like the sort of job that he would pass up cheerfully. Then, looking down at the frail figure on the porch steps, he had a thought.

If he refused, Cobb would probably find someone else. Someone quite willing to kill a couple of minors in return for a full poke and the thrill of it. It left him feeling oddly disoriented, as he followed the child' onto the porch and into a square parlor, whose high ceiling almost vibrated with the snortings of the sleeping man in the leather armchair.

Robert cleared his throat loudly. The snores changed pitch for a moment. Then they resumed their metronome-like regularity.

"You've got to shake him," said Andrew, his tone full of disgust. "He sleeps like a dead pig."

Robert was beginning to wish that he'd disregarded the letter with all its promises. He never had felt comfortable about waking sleeping people, and one who had a Colt revolver the size of his left leg on the table beside his hand was going to be trickier than most.

He moved quietly to the table and pushed the gun to the other side of the dusty surface. Then he bent low, touched the sleeping man's shoulder, and said, "Mr. Cobb! I'm Robert Evans. You wanted to talk with me?"

The child was gone as if he had never been, his step irregular as it thudded across the adjoining room. There was a series of snorts from Cobb. He gurgled, stretched, rubbed his eyes, and stood with a suddenness that sent Robert backward several paces.

"Who? What? And what might you be doing in my house?"

"I am Evans. Robert Evans. You wrote for me to come to see you. About a job."

The man sighed heavily and dropped into the armchair again. "Oh. Yes. Evans...otherwise known as...."

"Just Evans," said Robert, with some firmness. "The other name is lost in the past."

"Smart. They told me you was smart. So here you are, eh? Ready to go to work for Three Oaks. I thought you looked like somebody I could use."

"Hold on a minute, Mr. Cobb," Robert said. "I don't know what sort of job you want me to do. I don't know if it might suit me or not. We have to talk some first. Then we'll see."

Cobb stared at him, eyes filmed with sleep. His jaw dropped, then firmed up.

"I understood that you were somebody could do unusual things and keep your mouth shut afterward," he said.

"Unusual things, yes. I'm beginning to think that this one isn't all that unusual. I don't kill people, Cobb. I've broke about every other commandment, but that's one I've yet to smash."

Cobb blew his nose on a grimy handkerchief, polished the pair of glasses lying beside him on the table on the remaining

16

cleanish corner, and put them on to stare again at Evans.

"You're an outlaw. On the run. Wanted."

"Some might say so. You might say so, but by the time you got the chance, I'd be so far gone it wouldn't do you a bit of good. People don't blackmail me, Mr. Cobb. It goes the other way around."

Instead of being angry, Cobb snorted again, this time with laughter. "Feisty. I like that. I'll tell you what. I won't even say what the job will be till we size each other up. Then either you take it and stay, or you say no thank you and go."

Robert could see a wisp of uncombed hair showing above the window sill. Not Andrew's tow mop. Darker hair with a touch of auburn in it. Must be the brother, Kenneth, listening to his fate being decided in this unkempt room.

"Sounds fair enough," he said cautiously. "No hard feelings, either way?"

"No hard feelings," agreed Cobb. "Now let's go eat. That Mex'kin bitch ought to have supper ready by now. Sun's almost down."

The words sounded fine. But something was lacking in the tone. Robert had the uneasy feeling that it would not be as easy to decline Cobb's job offer as he had supposed. His unprotected back, across the miles of bare country between here and Dry Wells, would feel mightily exposed. It would be all too easy for anyone to put a bullet between his shoulder blades and never even be suspected.

They entered the big kitchen, and Cobb plunked himself down at the table. A haunch of venison steamed in a big iron vessel, flanked by potatoes and pinto beans. They smelled good, though the expression of the dark-haired woman at the stove should have curdled new milk.

She slapped a plate onto the wood before him, jangled a handful of tinware forks and knives and spoons into the middle of the table. "That all?" she asked. Her tone said that it had better be.

"Guess so. You be careful how you act around my guests, Quita. Now git. Your old man's prob'ly hollerin' right now."

Before she was out of earshot, Cobb said, "Can't train them greasers, no way you try. And her and her old man, they can't be run off the place, neither. My wife's sister was a fool and a ninny. Anybody would write a will like she did, and then get her man to agree to it, had to be out of their minds. Meléndezes! Greaser trash! Stuck with 'em forever, seems as if. The old man won't give way, sick or not."

Now the two boys had crept into the room, the older helping the younger, so his built-up shoe wouldn't clunk on the bare floor. They slipped into I heir places and began filling their plates, without a word spoken.

"You two! You washed up?"

They nodded, looking astonished. Robert suspected that never before had their semi-uncle showed any interest in such niceties.

"Try your best to raise 'em good, but it ain't easy. Kids can be a pain, you know that?"

Robert said nothing, just nodding as he chewed a mouthful of tender venison cooked to perfection, and followed that with a bite of mashed potatoes that could have floated off the plate. Quita, whatever her failings, could not number cooking as one of them.

When the meal was over, the boys disappeared with magical swiftness. Cobb seemed finished with his interview.

"Bunkhouse is out back. Plenty of room...we only got twenty hands, right now. Most of them're out in the hills, checking out yearlings. See you tomorrow."

Robert nodded. The dismissal was abrupt, even rude, but this was a man who seemed not to know any better. "I'll tell you tomorrow if I'll stay for a while," he said mildly. "Sometimes deals like that just don't pan out for either party. Sometimes they do. I'll sleep on it and let you know how I decide."

Cobb had started for his parlor again, but he jerked about and stared at Evans. His mouth opened, but before he could get a word out Robert had stepped out of the back door and was on his way toward the huddle of roofs that had to be the bunkhouse and equipment shed.

He found, when he reached that area, that one of the roofs covered a cookhouse. He could hear a mutter of talk and the clink of utensils against tin plates. Evidently Cobb preferred to have his hands fed at some distance from his own kitchen; aro-

18

matic smoke plumed from a stovepipe at one side of the ramshackle building. He smelled beans and bacon...he suspected that the hands seldom or never tasted the sort of fare Cobb put onto his own table.

Without pausing at the cook shed, Evans went toward a door that had to open into the bunkhouse. Inside was a long room lined with bunks on either side, with a shelf and washbasin at the end. The lack of a mirror told him that the others would probably be as unshaven as he. That was good...he wouldn't stand out as an oddity.

He looked at each bunk as he passed. Boots beneath, a shelf with odds and ends on the wall at the head warned him off the occupied ones. Halfway down the room, he found one whose blankets were still rolled tightly at the foot. No clutter of personal possessions occupied any of its space. He flung his pack onto the bunk and sat down to take off his boots.

He was halfway through washing in the tin basin when the men began to straggle into the room. They seemed unsurprised to find another hand in their midst, without any warning. Evidently Minta Granger had been correct when she said that the turnover was rapid.

As he dried his face on his own towel, scrubbing his beard between his hands to get the wet out, a lanky fellow whose head reached perilously near the low ceiling came over and nodded to him.

"New, eh? My name's Palmer. I ramrod. Old José's the straw boss, but he's gettin' a bit past the work. So I'm the one will be tellin' you what to do." The tone was relaxed and friendly, but Robert noted that the steel-gray eyes focused upon his face were assessing him coldly.

The man was a gunfighter. He'd met too many not to recognize the breed.

"I'm Bob Evans. Came in late this afternoon, and Mr. Cobb told me to come on down here. I haven't really took the job yet, but I'm thinkin' on it."

"Hope you stay," said Palmer. "We can't seem to keep men, and we run a lot of cattle. If we still had to make trail drives, we'd never be able to do it. The drive to the railhead isn't much, and we always seem to get it done short-handed."

19

None of the other men seemed interested in meeting him, so Robert stretched on his bunk and sighed contentedly.

"Been on the trail, eh?" asked the youngish fellow on the next bunk. He was shuffling a pack of worn cards, dealing, re-shuffling, re-dealing, as if practicing. Nobody seemed to want to come and sit on the end of his bunk to play with him.

Robert turned toward him, lying on his side. "Sure have. Six months, this time. Work's scarce where I been. If I wasn't so bone-tired, I'd play you a game of high-low."

"Oh, if you stay, there'll be plenty of time for that." The man smiled. His teeth were white and even, and his hands were not yet calloused with range work.

Gambler, said Robert's instinct. Just waiting to set up a new victim. Probably won all the wages these other chumps had for weeks, before they caught on.

Now what on God's green earth did Cobb want with a gun-slinger and a gambler? And if the first two so-called "hands" on this working ranch were such misfits, then what might the others be? He stiffened his resolve to leave in the morning, without making any agreement with the boss of this ridiculous outfit.

Closing his eyes, he turned onto his back again and pre-tended to drift off to sleep. But he was thinking hard. Some-thing about the way Minta Granger had said "we" when she mentioned doubting that Cobb treated his nephews well rang a warning bell. Probably the whole town had their eyes on Three Oaks, even if only from a distance.

Jebediah Cobb wasn't going to find it easy to get away with killing those boys, if that were so. He probably knew it, too. But how else did he plan to do the job?

Chewing on that bone of thought, Robert drifted off, de-spite the murmur of talk and the rattle of dice at the end of the room where the table sat.

CHAPTER THREE

Robert woke, as usual, before dawn. The faint sounds of the cook building the fire in the cookhouse stove across the way mingled with the groans and mutterings of the hands as they, too, fumbled their way from sleep to wakefulness. Though he had occupied many bunkhouses on many ranches across the width of the state, he had never found one with quite the feel of this one.

The men were too cautious. Usually a new hand was an occasion for rejoicing. He provided a new set of ears for the telling of old stories. His unknown capacities for gambling would provide a lot of entertainment, while the old-timers tried them out. He would be a source of news from other places and gossip, perhaps, about people some of them knew.

These men ignored him as they all dressed and washed (or some of them washed...several ignored that process) and moved grumpily toward breakfast. Sizing up the group, Robert found himself thinking that the only man he'd met since turning off the main road that he would trust farther than he could throw him had been old José.

The breakfast was ample, if uninspired. Toughish steaks, fried potatoes, flapjacks drenched in molasses made a filling meal against an active day. He wondered what Cobb was eating, up at the big house. But he ate in silence, listening to the occasional murmur of talk around the long table.

"Where's Ray? I wanted him to hunt out the calves over toward Grunt's Hill," Palmer was saying when Evans tuned in to him.

The very young man—no more than a boy, in fact—to whom he spoke looked uneasy. "The boss sent him out early this morning. Caught us when we came in from work and sent me on while he talked to Ray private. When I got up, Ray, he was long gone. Prob'ly some little thing Mr. Cobb needed doin'."

Robert's ears pricked up. Some little thing the boss needed doing might just include putting a slug in the back of someone who refused to take on the suspicious job he'd been brought here to do. He weighed the possibility against this urge to get out of Cobb's vicinity as soon as possible.

Palmer smiled. Robert was watching out of the corner of his eye, pretending to be absorbed in an account of a boar hunt in the hills that was being described across the table from him. He got the full benefit of the look of grim comprehension passing across the usually impassive face of the ramrod. So Palmer knew, or suspected, the errand that the missing Ray was to perform.

It would make sense to send someone out very early to cover the road out of the ranch. Robert wouldn't have known anyone was missing. He could have ridden out, after breakfast and telling Cobb his decision, and been followed through the rolling country until he was well on his way along the main road. And who would know, even if they suspected, that the murder had anything to do with Three Oaks Ranch?

Robert rose from the bench and handed his polished plate to the Chinese cook. "Good chow," he said politely.

The cook's black eyes regarded him thoughtfully. "You stay?" he asked. "Good grub we got, always." There seemed to be a warning, far back in the Oriental obscurity of the man's gaze.

"Oh, I think I'll stay for a while. Jobs're scarce. This looks like a pretty good place to work. At least until I get antsy again."

He purposely didn't look at Palmer. He strode out of the cookhouse and up toward the big house. Might as well tell Cobb he'd take on the job. If he was imagining things, it would soon come clear and he would leave. If he wasn't, he was covering his tail. And there was no way in hell Cobb could force him to do anything he objected to, though he wasn't about to admit that to the man. Let him think he had somebody who might help him with whatever his plot was regarding the boys. Even if Robert had intended to do anything to the poor kids before, he'd be on their side now. Who knew? It might do them some good.

The kitchen door was open, and he could see Quita moving around, putting away dishes into cupboards.

"Mr. Cobb up and around?" he asked, as she turned to see who had tapped on the doorframe.

"*Sí*. He is on porch. He wait for his horse. Always, he go out on range with the hands in morning. You go round house... see there?"

He followed her gesture around the bulk of the house, seeing for the first time how big and solidly built it was. The porch swing was creaking softly as he rounded the house, and he saw Cobb sitting there, pushing himself absently back and forth with one booted toe.

"Morning, Mr. Cobb," said Robert cheerfully. "I came up to tell you I think I'll work here for a bit. Get to know you and the situation. Then we can talk some more. All right with you?"

Cobb smiled. It didn't improve his piggy expression at all. "That sounds good to me. You just go ahead and settle in, work with the boys, meet José and Palmer. We've got a big operation here, and we always need good hands. I take it you've wrangled cattle before now?"

"There's no way to make it in this country without doing some of that, if you're not independently rich," said Robert. "Not to brag, but I'm a pretty good hand. Know one end of a horse from the other, and I can put a pretty neat brand on a calf's rump. Oh, I can pull my weight, Mr. Cobb, without anybody in the bunkhouse knowing I'm not just what I seem."

Cobb glanced toward the fence, where a young Mexican boy was opening the gate to lead in a big bay, barrel-chested and looking to have a good turn of speed. He seemed to lose interest in Robert.

"You go ahead, now. I'll call you up in a few days, see how you like things, see how you want to do things. I got to go, now.

"*Buen' días,* Arturo." All his attention was now for the horse, onto which he climbed with some difficulty. He was too heavy, it was plain, for either his own or the horse's comfort.

Robert grinned and turned back toward the corral, where he

had left his mount the night before. He needed a job, whatever sort it might turn out to be. If he could put a spoke in Cobb's wheel while making a bit of walking money, that would go down real easy.

CHAPTER FOUR

"Ken?" Andy's voice was low, though both boys knew their uncle was over at Flat Meadow, overseeing the branding of the six-month-old calves born there last spring.

The older boy turned his head a bit to look at his brother. "What?"

"That new fellow...I kind of liked him. Did you get to see him while he was in there with Cobb?"

"No. I heard what they said...he told Cobb right out that he wasn't any killer. Said he'd work here a while until Cobb told him what sort of job he wanted him for. Sounded like he meant what he said, but that don't mean a thing. You know that, Andy."

The smaller boy sighed. He was lying beside his brother in their favorite spot along the creek, hidden among the cotton-woods and doubly concealed by the overhang of the creek bank. They always waded along the narrow channel of water in the bottom of the creek to get here. So far, nobody had figured out their hiding place, when they didn't want to be found.

A jaybird lit above them and cocked his head down, fixing a shiny black eye toward them. His raucous cry rang through the narrow band of trees, but there was nobody there to hear him. Nobody who was an enemy, at least. Quita was in the yard, still doggedly trying to keep Mama's roses alive, but she'd never tell. Not even if she understood bird-talk.

"Is Cobb going to try to get somebody to kill us?" Andy's voice sounded a bit timid. "I don't want to die. Not even all broke up like I am. There's so much to see and do, out there. Where Miss Minta used to tell us about, when we could go in to town. Those books she'd read to us, when Mama let us spend the night with the Grangers, they just set me on fire to see oceans and cities and places across the water."

Ken set his chin onto his fist and stared down the shallow strip of water. Reflections danced over his high cheekbones, colored his hazel eyes.

"No, I don't think so. Even with Ma and Pa Granger gone, Miss Minta would keep our folks' friends in town on top of things. If we both was to be killed, all to once, she'd have the marshal out here like a shot. And if Cobb doesn't know that, he's dumber than I give him credit for.

"No, he's got something else up his sleeve. I can't quite figure it. That new fellow might be a part of his scheme, maybe. I can't see how, but don't trust nobody, Andy. Not anybody at all except for José and Quita."

"Why don't we just take off and walk out? We could make it, while Cobb is off on the range. Then we'd be safe and away from here. I know Miss Minta would take us in. She's our cousin, after all."

"Because we'd just get her into trouble and get ourselves watched so close we'd never get to do anything at all. The marshal's Cobb's old chum. It'd take somethin' like murder to get him charged up to make trouble for him. Don't you know Cobb would send some of those hard-cases down at the bunkhouse after us if we ran? And who knows what they'd try to do to Minta? No, we got to hang close and watch things. That's the only way I can figure for us to stay alive."

A shrill whistle sounded from the direction of the house. Quita. She covered for them as much as she could, and this was her prearranged signal that let them know to make sure they weren't caught doing anything their uncle objected to.

They slid down the creek bank and padded along the edge of the water, just deep enough so the current would scour away their footprints. They got to the place where they'd left their boots and had them on their feet in a rush. Then they picked up the switches they used for fishing poles, ran crickets onto the bent-pin hooks, and pretended to have been fishing for the few and tricky perch when their uncle strode heavily into the band of trees.

He seemed disappointed to find them innocently sitting on

the bank with their poles in their hands. "You kids come in to dinner. I got to go in to town, and we're eatin' early," he growled.

"Yes, sir," said Andres. He nudged Kenneth, who nodded. He closed his eyes to keep the hate from glaring forth like coals of fire.

The table was set with cold venison, pickles, sweet onions, and Quita's heavenly homemade bread. Sandwiches made with such ingredients should satisfy anybody, Andrew thought. Cobb, however, was livid.

"Good for nothin' Mex'kin!" he snapped at Quita. "Ought to have a big dinner on the table when I come in."

"If you tell me you come in, so I will do. You no tell me, you eat sandwich with the *niños* and like it," she snapped back.

Andrew hid his grin. Cobb never made any change off Quita. He didn't understand why the old man kept trying to needle her.

Daring, he said quietly, "I'd like to go into town, too. I haven't seen my cousin Minta Granger in almost a year. Take us with you, will you, Uncle?"

Cobb glared at him over the mug of coffee from which he was drinking. When he set the thing down, he banged it so hard on the table that brown liquid splashed.

"No, you can't go into town! You think I got nothin' better to do than nursemaid a couple of kids? I have business! You keep your mouth shut and stay out of my way." He glared at the boys, and they looked down at their plates and pretended to be busy with their food.

When he rode away on his bay, Kenneth spat into the dust where his tracks were printed. Andrew grinned. He understood what his brother was feeling.

CHAPTER FIVE

Robert had been riding for a long time before reaching Three Oaks, but the sort of work required for cutting out calves from beside their mothers was something needing reflexes and muscles used no place else in the world. He knew he was going to be sore the next morning. Still, he held his own, and he noticed that Palmer was keeping a sharp eye on him in the midst of the bawling calves and the frantic cows and the busy, dusty wranglers.

Palmer was more than he seemed to be, Evans was certain. If Meléndez could not be made to leave the ranch, still Palmer could be given the real authority over his motley crew of hands. There was no time to size up any more of the hard-bitten young men among whom he was working, but he suspected that Palmer himself, as well as Stinson, the gambler in the next bunk, were the rule, not the exception, here on Cobb's spread.

They worked the herd in Flat Meadows, taking two days to complete the job. Then Palmer led them into the hills west of Three Oaks. Robert found himself wondering how far even a forty-thousand-acre spread might stretch...it seemed to him that they had gone entirely too far.

He was convinced of that when he noticed that the grown animals in the herd they were approaching were branded with a "rocking T." No way in the world could you make that seem as if it were a plain C sitting on a crossbar. So Cobb was engaged in rustling his neighbor's young stuff, was he, as well as conspiring to get rid of the true owners of his own ranch?

Somehow it didn't surprise Evans in the least. It also explained the rag-tag bunch the man had in his bunkhouse. It made him a little uneasy, thinking of himself lumped in with the bunch of losers he worked with, though he kept arguing away with himself, inside his mind, all the time he cut out calves and roped and threw them for the iron.

"I am a fugitive from the law," he told himself. "No different, when you think of it, from any other. Not a bit better than Cold-Eye Palmer there, or Fingers Stimson or Pearly Kilpatrick. Why should it bother me to help steal a few calves? I hadn't a qualm in the world about bilking that banker in Nacogdoches out of his investments in my gold mine!"

Still, he felt odd, and that was the long and the short of it. That, possibly, is why he wasn't a bit surprised to look up about mid-afternoon to see a bunch of angry men come riding over the hill with blood in their eyes and guns in their hands.

Palmer saw them at just about the same time and let out a yell. "Head for home, boys!"

The crew took off, dropping branding irons and calves and leaping onto their horses with the skill .of a batch of acrobats. Robert would have been right in with them, except for the fact that he'd been engaged in tying a calf, and the animal had managed to involve him in the rope so he couldn't get loose with any speed at all.

He had his knife out, sawing at the strand, when the riders swept past and two horsemen peeled off and reined in their mounts on either side of him.

"Take it nice and easy," drawled the skinnier of the two. "We'd like to hang you, instead of shoot you. Mr. Tolliver's been losing stock for three years, right about this time of the summer. All young stuff that we haven't branded yet. So now we know. Tough. You're goin' to have to stand in for the whole entire gang."

Robert, strangely, wasn't too disturbed. He had not yet seen a situation he couldn't talk his way out of, and he suspected that this one wasn't going to be the exception.

"Tolliver? I guess I haven't been here long enough to recognize the name. Just worked for Cobb three days, now. I hadn't any idea these weren't his cattle. I'm just a hired hand."

"Cobb?" This voice came from behind him, and he turned to see a fat man on a fat white mare coming back from the direction in which the pursuers had gone. "Jebediah Cobb?"

Robert allowed himself to look as surprised as he felt. "Why sure. Jebediah Cobb, the man I went to work for on Monday. The man whose ramrod told us we were out here on Mr. Cobb's place to brand the spring calf crop."

Under the white hair straggling beneath the hat-brim, the round face went even redder than repeated blisterings and weatherings could account for. "Don't try to lie to me, boy. I know this gang's been raiding herds all around here for years, now. Cobb may be a mean, unsociable old brute, but he's no cattle thief. You're goin' to hang, makes no difference, so's there's no reason to try puttin' a man's neck in the noose along with yours."

Robert smiled. Then he began to laugh. The three horsemen looked puzzled as they stared down at their unorthodox candidate for the noose.

"What's so funny?" asked Tolliver.

"You poor dodos thinking there's some extra-smart gang of owlhoots takin' your young stuff, and all the time it's your own neighbor! A joke like that's worth hangin' for!" he gasped.

Tolliver frowned. He looked sharply at Evans before turning to one of his men. "Tie him up and bring him to the house. We'll get to the bottom of this before we fit him out for a tight necktie."

The rope was cut off the calf and used to complete his own entanglement. Robert found himself mounted on his own horse, which was led by the skinny man, whose name turned out to be Sim. They went up the slope to the northwest and found themselves in a maze of choppy hills spotted with patches of oak scrub. Cattle trails cobwebbed off in all directions, but the old man knew exactly where he was going and led then down and around and over hills, across a creek, up a slope covered with sun-killed grass, and down into a shady cup rimmed with locust and cottonwood trees.

The house was almost hidden in a thick growth of shrubbery, rose vines, and flower beds. A short, pink woman waited on the porch as the four horses were pulled up at the hedge forming a front fence.

"Who's that, Hiram?" she asked, as Sim and his friend Lunt pulled Robert from his mount and shoved him through the gap in the hedge.

"Rustler. Claims to work for Cobb, but I know better. Got to get to the bottom of it, though, before we hang him."

She clucked softly to herself. "Now Hi, come on in and drink some coffee and think about things before you go off half-cocked. You recall that Mexican you hung three years ago? Turned out he was just lost and lookin' for directions. We've been stuck with takin' care of his family ever since. Don't you go getting us in Dutch again!"

Tolliver snorted and turned turkey-wattle purple. But he dismounted stiffly and trudged off toward the house, leaving his henchmen to bring Robert in behind him.

A coffee-pot that could have held two gallons of liquid sat on the back of the iron cook stove. Steam rose gently from its spout, and Robert suspected that it simmered all day every day, its contents getting stronger and stronger until a pebble would have bounced off its surface.

The woman poured the black stuff into thick mugs, setting one beside the spot where he had been pushed into a chair by his guards. "Here, you all drink this and then start talking about things like sensible people. Hi, what makes you think Jebediah Cobb wouldn't steal? I'd be real interested to know."

Her husband took a long pull at the mug. Robert followed suit, holding the cup between bound hands. He wondered why his teeth didn't melt. He breathed between clenched teeth, trying to cool his scalded tongue as well as to dissipate the bitterness.

Tolliver set his mug down and stared at Robert. "Can you offer me any proof that you work, have worked, or might possibly work in the future for Jebediah Cobb?" he asked, his tone sarcastic.

"Of course," said Robert. "If one of these fellows will pull my wallet out of my hip pocked, I'll show you the letter I got from him. It's dated a while back, but I've been moving around, and it just got to me about six weeks ago."

Sim, without being told, fumbled at his hip pocket, while Robert leaned forward. Out came the worn wallet. The false identification was in it and little more. It had been a scanty year, this past one. But tucked into the flap at the back was the letter from Cobb. Robert thanked his stars that only one looking between the lines could have seen the faintly disturbing tone of the thing.

Tolliver took a pair of wire-rimmed spectacles from the pocket of his overalls and put them on. He read aloud:

Dear Mr. Evans,

As I find myself needing someone to help me with an unusual project, I am venturing to send this letter by way of mutual acquaintances, asking that you come to visit me on my forty-thousand acre ranch near Dry Wells, Texas. I have heard of your unique skills. I find that a person of your talents may be useful to me, in the pursuit of my short-term goals.

I hope that you will consent to visit Three Oaks Ranch, in order to discuss your possible employment here. I hope that this catches up with you fairly soon and that you will come at all possible speed, once it does.

Most sincerely yours,
Jebediah Cobb

Tolliver stared over his glasses. "What unusual skills?"

Robert, for once in his life, was taken aback. To be at a loss for words was astonishing, and he stared back, his mind turning at top speed. But nothing came to mind except the unvarnished truth.

"I'm a con-man," he said. "I think Cobb thought I was a killer, but I'm not. Just a con-man."

"Sara," said the old man, turning to his wife, "the boys!"

They drew back as if Robert might be something poisonous.

"Hey!" he protested. "I'm no killer, I told you that. I've already told him I won't kill his nephews."

"Then why are you still hanging around Three Oaks?" asked Sara.

"Because I have a crazy feeling that if I try to leave, a man called Ray...I've never met him...may try to backshoot me on the road."

She moved to stand beside her husband. He looked up, nodded slowly, and surveyed his captive with a new sort of interest.

"Then maybe," said Hiram Tolliver, "we may not have to hang you, after all."

CHAPTER SIX

As a matter of principle, Robert had spent the better part of his twenty-eight years avoiding even the .semblance of legal activity. Given the choice between cooperating with Tolliver's scheme for catching his neighbor red-handed or hanging from the cottonwood beyond the Tolliver front door, he altered the habits of a lifetime with commendable speed.

That, of course, was not the end of it. He had to look as if he had escaped from his captors with great difficulty and danger. He felt that Sim and Lunt had put a bit more vigor into their efforts to make him look convincing than was absolutely necessary. As he crawled through the scrub, leading the unsaddled mount he was supposed to have stolen for his getaway, he decided that the right side of the law might possibly be even less comfortable than the wrong side.

Every bone ached. His teeth felt loose, and one gum kept bleeding. His right eye was almost shut, as well, and the left was puffy with bruises. When he inhaled deeply, he felt a sharp pain, as if a rib might have cracked when Sim let him have the last of his supposedly simulated blows.

It was agony to ride the horse. The bony back scrubbed all the muscles that he had known were going to be sore from his unaccustomed work all week. But walking across this endless country was something you didn't do...particularly in working boots, whose high heels dug into the dry soil and whose tops tended to irritate the calves of your legs. They were not intended for walking.

Lunt had drawn him a map. That was the only reason he'd been able to find his way through the maze of rounded hills, oak scrub, dry washes, and dried-out grasslands lying between the

Rocking T and Three Oaks. He'd have wandered around until he left his bones to dry out along with the rest of the terrain, without it. And now he was approaching the creek, down whose course he would find Cobb's house, his nephews, Cold-Eye Palmer, and possibly the unknown Ray.

It had been two days since he left his captors. Though Mrs. Tolliver had protested heartily, Tolliver and his men insisted that Robert be given only the scantiest rations, so he would look properly lank when he arrived at his destination. Robert had to admire the thought for detail, but his belly felt as if it might be permanently stuck to his backbone.

The cottonwood shade, however, felt wonderfully cool. The trickle of water in the creek, while not particularly clear and tempting, was at least wet, and he was grateful for it. Tolliver had refused to give him a canteen.

"You might forget and keep it till you get there. And besides, you'd look entirely too frisky and juicy, if you'd of been drinkin' well all the way. No, two days'll see you through, and if you fill up good here, you can make it to the creek," Hiram had said. He was right, of course, but Robert would have settled for less artistic thoroughness.

He had made it to the creek, of course, but he still felt as if he'd never get his back teeth wet. And now he was staggering down the watercourse, having made it past the scrubby patch, and in the distance he could see a plume of smoke rising high. From Quita's kitchen fire, he suspected, or the Chinaman's cookhouse.

He dropped the line by which he led the horse. It had been made from strips torn from his shirt-tail and added, he thought, another bit of verisimilitude to his story. The beast followed him, as he had known it would. Neither horse nor man took kindly to being completely alone.

He was splashing a bit as he went down the edge of the water. He was truly dizzy with hunger, and his bruises and contusions were making him grit his teeth in order to keep moving. Still, he had given Tolliver his word, and even a word given under threat of hanging was sacred to an Evans...no! A Willingham. He was getting confused. He hears something up ahead. Splashing. Voices. He gave a feeble yell.

"Hey! Hey! Come help me!" It sounded as desperate as he would have wanted it to be, but he was just that desperate and it wasn't acting.

He went to his knees amid the damp pebbles of the stream-bed. The horse nickered softly, nosing the back of his neck. "Hey!" he croaked.

Then, adding just the right touch to the scenario, he passed out.

* * * * * * *

He came to lying on his bunk. Quita was standing beside him, looking down with clinical concern. He realized to his horror that he was buck naked under the blanket, though he was also clean. The grit that had accompanied him for the past weeks was gone.

He tried to move, but it hurt so abominably that he settled back with a groan. "How'd I get here?" he asked, finding it hard to make his voice behave.

"The boys, they find you up the creek. Mr. Cobb, he very upset. When you are able to walk, he will see you at house. But for now, you rest. Better tomorrow. Bao, he know very good liniment for bruise. Nothing broke, so you back at work soon."

With that comforting thought, she nodded decisively and left the bunkhouse. As if she had driven them all out (which she probably had, he realized) the men straggled back and made some excuse to pass his bunk and stare down at him. After a time, Palmer joined them, motioned the rest away, and sat down on Stinson's bunk.

"So what happened?" he asked, his eyes still cold and suspicious. "How'd you manage to get away from that bunch? Tolliver's tough and he can be real mean when he loses his temper."

Robert sighed, but it hurt, so he decided not to take a deep breath again until his ribs healed better.

"I was all tangled up with that heifer, so they got me cold," he said. It hurt, so he rested a moment before continuing. "The two skinny guys wanted to string me up right there and then, but the old man rode up and said to take me to the house. I dunno why. So they tied me up and slung me on my horse. I've lost him for good, this time, I'd bet on it." He rested again.

"What did he want?" asked Palmer, leaning forward, his gaze intent. "Did he ask you any questions about...cattle rustling?"

"Course he did. He thought I was a member of a super-smart gang that worked this range every summer. I didn't tell him anything. Figured they was going to hang me anyway, so there wasn't any sense in getting anybody else into trouble. I wasn't bein' noble," he added, seeing the doubt in Palmer's eyes. "Just sensible."

Now he was at the point at which the carefully worked out story Tolliver had concocted began, so he went slowly. "The one they called Sim went to take my wallet out of my pocket. That made me sweat, 'cause Mr. Cobb's letter was inside. He got between me and Lunt, the other one, and both of 'em was between me'n the old man, Tolliver. I'd managed to loose up my hands while we was riding. So I grabbed Sim and got his gun."

"So when did they beat you up?"

"Oh, they did that while we was passin' the time of day, right after they caught me. Tolliver stopped 'em. It didn't make jumpin' Sim any easier, I guarantee."

"And where did you get the horse?"

Robert grinned painfully. "Out of the pasture east of the house. While the three of 'em was running around, getting rifles and peppering away at the cottonwood and locust trees, I was skitin' up the creek and crossin' over toward the way we'd come. I knew if I lost my bearings in this crazy country I'd never find my way back here.

"This old nag was grazing over by itself, so I just hauled myself aboard and took off. I doubt if Tolliver even knows it's gone, yet. It don't look like his best piece of horseflesh, now does it?"

Palmer stared out the window toward the corral. "Can't say it does." His tone was still guarded.

When he looked back down at Robert, he said, "And is that letter still in your wallet?"

"Seeing as nobody ever got a hand on it, and I haven't had

time to think about it since, I 'spect it is," said Evans.

He turned his head with some effort to look at the shelf where his belongings should be. He could see the corner of his wallet sticking over the edge. "Up there, I guess."

Palmer took the wallet and peeled back the flap. The letter was there, creased and grimy, just as Tolliver had put it.

"Thanks for havin' somebody to clean me up and fix up the bad spots," said Robert. "I'm not easy, but I'd have been a sight worse without it."

Palmer peeled his lips away from his teeth in his forbidding grin. "Oh, we didn't tend to you. Quita did. She can do it pretty good, that gal. Said you looked like hamburger, too. Cobb was sort of wonderin' if Tolliver might not have sent you back as a spy, till she told him that."

Robert began to have a better regard for Tolliver's artistic details. "I could've just gone on," he said, his tone mild. "But I came back here because I need a job."

Palmer closed his mouth into its usual steel trap line. "Then I think you may just have one. Not wranglin'. Cobb's got...special needs. You just may be the one he's been wanting to take care of 'em."

Robert couldn't quite decide which bothered him most—being undressed and washed like a baby by the black-eyed Quita or finding himself Jebediah Cobb's right-hand man. Before he could decide, he drifted off to sleep.

CHAPTER SEVEN

Every Tuesday morning, Quita hitched the feisty black horse belonging to her father to the buggy that had belonged to Cobb's wife and, before her, to his late sister-in-law. She took a big market basket, a Colt half as long as she was, and headed for Dry Wells.

Mail was, of course, the principal item of interest, though little came addressed to Three Oaks Ranch. Supplies were hauled in by wagon once a month, so she wasn't really obliged to pick up items for Cobb's table. Gossip and female companionship, however, were not obtainable in any other way, and Quita had made it plain to Cobb that she went with or without his permission. On Tuesdays, he had to suffer with the boys' cooking.

On this particular Tuesday, however, Quita had more than her usual budget of information to trade with Minta Granger and the women at the Catholic Church on the south road. She had been keeping her eyes and ears alert, over the past year, for any hint that Cobb might be a threat to his wife's nephews. Now she felt that she had good reason for worry about the boys.

She pulled up at the store/post office and called to Minta, even before hitching the black.

"Mees Granger? You see, las' week, a man come through? Ask for Three Oaks, maybe?"

Minta came to the door. Winthrop, eyes half-closed, followed her meekly onto the porch and stood beside her like some unlikely bodyguard.

"Quita! Come in! Yes, I did meet a fellow last week—Evans, his name was. Said he had a job out there. Blond beard? Middle-sized? Not very big?"

"The same." Quita took her basket from the buggy and climbed the steps onto the porch. "I think he have come to hurt Kenny and Andy."

"He didn't look dangerous to me. Had sort of a sly look in his eye, but I didn't get the feeling he might be a killer, though Lord knows, Jebediah Cobb wouldn't be past doing in those boys to get their property into his own name. Here, sit down and tell me why you're worried."

Quita perched on the leather-bottomed chair while Minta took the wooden bench along the wall. She seemed hard put to begin, but at last she said, "Cobb, he look much too please' with himself since Evans come. And something else happen—I do not know how to say what it mean. Perhaps you are able?"

"Evans get hurt, last week. He go out with crew for brand calves. Crew come back, all upset and angry, but Evans not with them. Cobb, he very upset. Curse and stamp around and hit boys. I keep very still; don't go home when time come...just creep back up along creek to watch.

"Cobb and that bad man Palmer have long talk on porch. I cannot hear, but they look very serious and worried. That happen on Wednesday. Evans not there for two days. Then Palmer come to me, say, 'Got a man hurt. You fix him up!' And I go, and it is Evans, all beaten. Very thin, sunburned, bruised and cut and probably have crack' ribs."

Minta stared at her, dark eyes round. "He looked as if he had been beaten?"

"*Sí*. Very bad beaten. Tied, too...rope leave marks on wrists. Palmer say he be thrown from horse, lost, they been search. That is a lie. Nobody have search' at all. I see them all for two days, go about business like nothing wrong." She shifted uneasily on the chair.

"Sunday Evans come to house. Still limp, but he been work on Saturday. Cobb take him into study, close door, leave Stinson in hall to see nobody Listen. When Evans come out, Cobb also come, smile all over face. Very happy, Cobb is now. Too happy. When bad man happy, good man weep, my father say."

Minta nodded. "José knows what he's talking about. The Town council meets tomorrow at the Methodist church. I'll bring this up then...we have all had an eye on Cobb ever since Letitia died...was killed. I never did think that was an accident. That man Palmer was riding with her when the thing happened. I wouldn't put anything past him, but we've never been able to prove a thing."

"Palmer bite rattlesnake, snake get very sick. Maybe die," said Quita in a sad tone. "My father, he think so, too. He keep watch, but he very sick now. Sit up all night with pain in belly. But he ride, too. They not know...he keep our string in our own corral. Too far for Palmer or Cobb to keep track of how we use our own horse."

"And Evans...how did he act, after his talk with Cobb?" asked Minta. She was twirling a bit of twine about her finger, untwisting it, winding it tight again. Quita knew that she was thinking hard.

"Evans, he take things very easy. He go right back to work, never say anything, never talk much to other hands. He stay right away from Palmer, but I don't find out why. The boys... they like him. That scare me."

Minta looked concerned. "It scares me, too. If he should take them for a ride out on the range and there should be an accident, who could prove anything? I'll tell Dr. Duncan and Mayor Long what you've said, Quita. I had a funny feeling when Evans rode in here last week. He seemed likable enough, but he kept reminding me of somebody, and I never did pin it down, though I had the feeling it wasn't anybody really nice."

She gazed down the dusty street, which sported a tumbledown livery stable, the café-saloon-boarding-house, the Methodist church, the Catholic church, and the Baptist church, side by side in the trees beyond the town proper. At the side of the livery stable was a cube of a building that housed Mayor Long in his incarnation as the only lawyer within fifty miles. Only the railhead at Lawson possessed another in his line of work.

Doctor Duncan worked out of his rambling frame house that was out of sight beyond the churches. He often joked that it was convenient having his place of business so close to the cemetery, though those honest enough to admit it knew that he cured a lot more people than he killed.

Quita rose to go into the store. "I think Cobb like something different," she said. "You got something different?"

"Three different kinds of dried beans," said Minta, her tone dry. "We did get some canned pears in the other day. See if you can hook him on those. And a hoop of cheese that could walk off by itself. Look around, Quita. When you've through, write down what you took, and I'll put it on Cobb's bill. I've got to go down to talk to Mayor Long right now. I think he needs to know what you've told me."

She left Quita browsing among the dusty shelves. The Mexican girl watched her go, then busied herself with trying to please her difficult employer's demanding appetite. The one thing he wanted from her that might accomplish that was something she refused to think about. She had made the error of telling her father, some weeks ago, that Cobb wanted her to move into the house as his housekeeper-mistress, and she still shivered at the fury she had read in his pain-filled eyes.

"You take care," he had told her. "Do not go near him, if you can help. Do not be alone with him, if it is possible. Ask Kenneth to stay close...he will understand. That is bright boy. Grown enough to understand. I will talk with him, too."

He must have done it, too, for Quita had found it comforting to find the older boy hanging so close about her heels. She had found that she felt more secure when Evans was about the house, also, though that made her feel strange. If he was a killer, why did she like him so much?

CHAPTER EIGHT

Robert was in a bind. He had been in tight places, of course, all his life, but there had always been some loophole out of which he saw a way to wriggle. Not this time. The invisible Ray had been detailed to shoot him if he tried leaving the ranch alone. Bao had told him that.

The little Chinaman had, for some inscrutable Oriental reason, taken a liking to him. He saved food for him when he was late getting back after a day's work. He sought out opportunities to talk with him, if it seemed private enough so nobody suspected what he was doing.

The warning had come the afternoon after his interview with Cobb. Bao waited until the other hands had gone off to do the chores saved for Sundays. Then he crept into the bunkhouse and approached the bunk, where Robert lay nursing his collection of aches.

"You be careful," said the little man. "I see you go to house. Talk to Cobb, I know. He have ugly job for you? Kill boy?"

Robert shook his head...too hard. He suppressed a groan as he said, "No. I told him up front that I'm no killer. It's...something else he wants me to do. Maybe worse." He didn't know why he'd added that, except that it seemed a lot worse to him than a clean killing.

"Worse than kill?" Bao sounded skeptical.

"Believe me, you'd think so too if I told you. But I don't think you want to know. Cobb's suspicious of his own left toes. You don't want to know anything you might let drop."

"You don't want to do job. I see that. You no bad man, hurt young boy. So now I tell you—you not run away. Not in day, not in night. You see Ray yet?"

Robert shook his head, very gently.

"He out there, wait for you to run. Palmer send him. I hear, out behind cook shed while I empty ash. Say kill you if you leave alone. You know too much, he say. Only way you quit Three Oaks is dead. "

"Why are you tellin' me all this?" asked Robert. "You don't owe me anything."

"No. But I do owe boys' parents. They treat me good, help family, give me job. If Cobb think you do the thing he want, he not get other man to do it, you see? Other man might go ahead. Maybe you find way to make boy safe."

Robert chuckled softly. "You read my mind, you old devil. How did you know that was what I was planning to do?"

"Bao read man pretty good," he said. His black eyes were amused. "People here think we talk like child, we think like child. Not so. I read Cobb. I read you. I read Palmer." He wrinkled his mouth with disgust. "You only man on ranch, except José, will help those boy. You help!"

Though Robert was working several days a week with the crew, in order to maintain some pretense of legitimate employment, he was also spending the rest of his free time with Kenneth and Andrew. The more he saw of the pair, the more he hated their uncle. The two had been bullied almost out of their minds, though they retained enough spunk to indulge in small rebellions from time to time.

He took them on long rides over the range, feeling all the while an unseen gaze focused on his back and an invisible rifle aimed at him by Ray's hidden hands. The boys loved those jaunts. To be allowed to ride, after being denied for so long, was a joy to both.

"Mama and Papa had ponies for us, when we were little," Andy said. "We rode together a lot. But when the storm came, and Aunt Lettie came to take care of us, she was afraid of horses. So she wouldn't let us ride, even with José. And Cobb thinks all our horses belong to him. He won't even let us go to the corral, unless he has some job he wants us to do."

While Andy talked, Robert watched Ken. The boy's eyes were too veiled for someone his age, too wary. He took a long while in sizing up his new companion, and Robert relaxed and let things ride.

"How can I drive 'em crazy right off the bat?" he asked Cobb, when the man urged him to speed.

"You have to get right in where people live to do that. Somebody you don't know or care about can't get that close to you. If I'm going to get those boys committed to the crazy house, it's going to take time, and you might as well make up your mind to that."

He had nightmares when he thought too much about the task he had been set. Putting two bright, active children into an insane asylum, so their uncle could get permanent custody of them and their property, was something that made him feel sick inside. Even though he was trying to find an angle that would blow things apart, once he and the kids were safely out, he worried a lot.

He wondered about approaching José or Quita, but Palmer watched him or had him watched closely all the while he was near the ranch house. Bao found no more opportunity to communicate with him, though he sometimes grunted a greeting as Robert went into the cookhouse.

It was a dilemma. Robert found the intelligence that he thought he had left back East coming to his aid, somewhat to his surprise. The law degree he had worked on, thinking all the while he'd never use any part of the dull information, might just come in handy, after all. He knew something about law. He could get the proper papers in order for Cobb. That was no problem. Could he also build into them some sort of self-destruct that was subtle enough not to strike the notice of a judge or Cobb's lawyer? Something that, if challenged, would let the boys go free?

As he puzzled and worried, he got to know the boys better and better. Even Ken began to warm up to him, as he racked his brain for fun things to do with the children. Quita packed picnics and they rode up the creek to fish and eat and laze in the shade, talking about the sorts of things that boys wonder about.

These boys, he found, wondered more than most, lacking as they did any parent at all. Robert found himself resenting Cobb fiercely.

45

He came to resent the absent Ray even more fiercely. Being pinned down, without a visible danger to cope with, was something he wasn't used to and didn't like even a little bit. He had behaved so meekly so far that he wondered if Ray might not be getting a little slack.

That notion stayed with him for another couple of weeks. Let the fellow get complacent. Let him begin dozing in his hidey hole. That was fine.

For Robert intended to do something about Ray. Very soon, and very permanently.

CHAPTER NINE

A plan was forming, slowly but solidly, in Robert's mind. While he mulled it over, he was also considering ways in which he might satisfy his ambitions concerning Ray. The man was evidently the hardy sort who didn't mind sleeping out and eating scantily. There was no sign that he approached the bunkhouse, the cookhouse, or even the big house, though Robert couldn't keep close watch on all those.

He asked Kenneth about Ray, as they sat on the creek bank, watching Andrew pitching pebbles into the eddy beyond the bend. "I keep hearing about him, but I've never seen hide nor hair of him. Is he real?"

Kenneth didn't laugh, though he now recognized Robert's teasing moods and usually entered into the spirit of fun. "He's... creepy. Cobb hired him before Aunt Lettie died. She didn't like him a bit, and he stayed away from her as much as he could. She kept after Cobb to let him go, but he wouldn't do it. And after the accident, Cobb talked and talked to Ray. He was at the house most all the time."

"But what sort of man is he? Where did he come from? And does he have a last name?" Robert asked.

"He's...mean, I guess. Looks like he never smiled in his life. Black hair, mud-colored eyes. His last name is Peters, he says but Andy and I think he's on the run and it's something different. He never mentions any place he came from. Sometimes he disappears for a long time, and Cobb says he's on business for the ranch. But we get a funny feeling about that."

Andrew, back still turned to them, said, "He tried to cut Winthrop's throat once. Miss Minta near had a fit. Winthrop butted Ray right off the porch of the store. Got his clothes dusty. Bruised his nose. Ray pulled a knife out of his boot and caught Winthrop from behind. He'd have cut him, if Miss Minta hadn't beat him off with her broom handle. She told him if he ever came back to Dry Wells she'd shoot him. I don't think he's ever been back, either. He sends Stinson after his tobacco and fixin's."

Robert had a vivid mental picture of the formidable Miss Granger attacking this bugaboo with a broom-handle. It took some of the aura of danger away, that was certain. "So he's afraid of Miss Granger, is he?" he asked in an amused tone.

"And Palmer is afraid of him." That was Kenneth, his voice entirely too serious for someone his age. "Palmer turns pale when Ray looks at him."

The exchange had left Robert thoughtful for days. Still, he had to do something, just for his own peace of mind. So when the moon was dark, the range almost crackling aloud with drought, he eased himself out of his bunk along about midnight. The bunkhouse was a symphony of snorts and buzzes and zooming snores. From time to time, someone down at the end of the row of bunks gave hollow groan, as if he were dreaming of being tortured by Indians. Robert had learned to recognize every night-sound made by all his companions. Palmer's light breaths, hinting at instant awakening at need; Stinson's burring snore; every intonation and all the variations of every man in the place was now in the Evans' repertory.

They were all sounding off, steady as clockwork. 'He lowered himself to hands and toes and tickled his way down the aisle as lightly as a spider, his clothing tight in a bundle against his back. He didn't go to the door. If anything was watched at night, that would be it. He eased around the sharp corner into the equipment room. When the door was silently shut behind him, he began to breathe again for himself.

His shirt and pants went on, and the moccasins be intended to use slid onto his feet. He'd left his gun and ammunition, as well as his big knife, in the pack on his peg in the shed where his saddle hung. He had a feeling that this night would see the end of his career as a peaceful con-man.

The window of the equipment room was unglazed, a simple shutter affair secured on the inside with pegs. He had it open, was out, and had pushed it tightly shut again within seconds. He had scouted the outside of the bunkhouse carefully, pretending to be looking for a cartridge that had bounced away from him. Now his soft-clad feet felt their way surely over the dry soil. The shed and his weapons loomed up against the dark sky, even darker in angular bulk.

He didn't bother with saddle or horse. Once he was armed, he set out at a light trot over the terrain east of the ranch. The road was off to his right, he knew. He had memorized the irregular contours of the hills, and he kept his bearings pretty well as he moved into the rolling country between the house and the main road.

Ray was (he hoped) human. He'd surely have something going. A little fire. A cigarette. Even a sigh from time to time. If he was there, Robert knew he'd find him. His senses were homed to incredible sharpness by the darkness and the danger of his errand. He had to get his human watchdog and return to his bunk before get-up time.

Once he was well into the heaving rolls of land, he slowed to a cautious walk, his steps silent, even on the dried grass and the cracked soil. Now it was up to his ears, and he blessed the years of training that would now help him to remove his nemesis. He might leave or he might not. Either way, he didn't intend to be coerced.

The wind was sighing through the dried stubble grass. Somewhere, a horse was trying to graze. Robert, pausing, heard even the brittle roots of his mouthfuls tear away from the dusty soil. A horse, here, meant a man. The string for the ranch was kept in the greener country along the creek. A man had to mean Ray.

Robert prudently dropped again to his stomach. He hoped he wouldn't find himself nose-to-nose with a sidewinder as he scuttled over the rough terrain. That, however, just had to be a chance he took.

He moved up a long, shallow slope, going toward the sound of the horse. From time to time the beast shifted his ground, his hooves thudding lightly in the dust. It whickered softly, once in a while, and he could hear, in the stillness of the night, the swish of its tail. It made a good point to home in on.

He came over the rise as nearly flat as a man can get and still move at all, even crawling, He prided himself on the fact that he made far less sound than the beast ahead of him. Even the grass didn't crackle as he slid over it. He paused beneath the skyline and risked an eye's width above the line of terrain.

And then he froze, stunned. Something completely unexpected was going on in the small hollow between two rolls of land.

CHAPTER TEN

There was a tiny flicker of coals in the cup. In such a dark night, it lit the scene well enough. Too well. For three Indians had the man Robert was hunting, and they looked to be set for a long hard evening.

Even as he watched, one of the dark-skinned men below him pushed a pile of dried dung onto the coals, which sprang into a brisk blaze. By that light, Robert could see that these were Comanche, a long way from their home grounds. They were not decked out for war, as far as he could tell, but they looked grim and businesslike.

He desperately wanted to know what was taking place, but he also knew his Comanche. They were alert for anything and nothing, and getting past them was not a thing most men would like to try. Yet he had risked the sidewinders. He might as well risk the Indians as well. He crept forward a fraction of an inch at a time.

The ridge along which he moved curved sharply inward, and he followed it until he was just above the group below. He saw the standing Indian plainly in the firelight, though the other two seemed content to look on from the shadows. Clad in leggings and breechclout, his shoulders covered scantily by a tom cotton shirt that had been bright red but was now streaked with faded strips, the Indian was staring down at Ray Peters.

Robert stared, too. He had been haunted by the specter of this man for the weeks he had been Three Oaks. Now there he was, and something about the flat glare of his eyes made Evans shiver. Ray had the same look about him that the sidewinder would have...a soulless chill that would make killing just a part of a normal day.

51

Robert wondered suddenly how he would have fared if he had been the one to creep silently into this cup of land and tackle Ray in his camp. He felt suddenly cold.

"You work for Jebediah Cobb?" The voice startled Robert, and the cultured turn of the English words surprised him.

Ray drew his lips back from his teeth, reminding Robert of Palmer's trick. "Maybe I do, maybe I don't," he growled. "I don't talk to no Injuns."

"I suspect that you will talk with me," said the man by the fire. "I intend that you should. I have a bone to pick with Cobb, and I have no objection to picking your bones to learn what I want to know." He stared down at the guard, and now Robert could see that Ray was tied firmly, hand and foot.

"I will first tell you a small tale, so that you can understand my seriousness. Two years ago, my family was on our yearly hunt into the southern lands. We had killed our deer, dressed them, and were on our way home with the meat. This ranch lies across our ancient hunting road, and we followed it. The people who claimed this land never objected to that. We always gave them venison, and they were grateful." Robert could see the lines on that dark face, the wrinkles at the corners of the black eyes deepen.

"Things had changed, and we did not know that. We went south with a band of our people, moving east of this place. We returned by our old road. And Cobb sent out men, who shot my horses, raped my women, and killed my son."

Robert felt a cold finger run down his backbone. No wonder the old Indian was out for blood. The only wonder was that he had waited for two years.

"They shot me, many times. I crawled away, after they left me for dead. I lived...anger and hatred filled me, and I could not die. I was found by a young man of my tribe and taken home again, where I have spent two years in regaining my strength. The hatred has not died. And now I am here again. I want Cobb. Tell me about him."

"How come you talk like some goddamned professor and not like a proper Injun?" asked Ray. It was not a question that would have occurred to Robert. Not in the present circumstances.

A grunt of guttural laughter came to his ears. "I went to a mission school, of course. I learned the language and rejected the weakling's religion." He stepped close to the recumbent man and touched his side with the toe of a moccasin.

"Where were you, two years ago?" came the question. It had the chilling quality of a snake's hiss.

"Why right here on Three Oaks, where I'd been a few months. I'd already done a job for the old man. Killed his old lady, in fact. You sure had a couple of pretty squaws. If they hadn't of died so quick, I'd of had another go at 'em." Ray smirked, his expression clear in the brightness of the dung fire.

It was, of course, insanity. Robert, hidden beyond the ridge, understood that all too well. But the man down there seemed to have no human feelings, not even those of fear or caution.

Evans lay flat, feeling as if those black eyes might see him even through the darkness. What was going to happen to Ray, now, he knew too well. Once he had been caught in the same trap, and only luck and his quick wits had pulled him out of it. There was no such escape for Ray. He wouldn't have saved the man if he could. Let the Comanche do the work he had come to do. He slid backward, silent, tense, listening for any sign of interest beyond the hill.

From behind him came a hiss of pain. Ray's, of course. By the time he reached the wrinkled map of draws and swells on the ranch-side of his hiding place, even Ray was howling like a banshee. It made Robert flinch. He had known the kiss of hot iron on his own skin. He had been marked with a sharp knife by those who did not have his welfare at heart.

He didn't envy Ray. And, by God, he didn't pity him, either. A man who would kill a woman just so her husband could steal her nephews' property was so much horse dung, better off forgotten.

But those long-drawn cries followed him as he made tracks back toward the bunkhouse. He now had two dilemmas. What to do about the boys was, of course, the most important. But the other had some personal elements. Should he warn Palmer or Cobb that there were Comanche on the land, and Comanche with blood in their eyes?

CHAPTER ELEVEN

The stars seemed to be sitting on top of him, glaring as if to betray Robert to any eye scanning the countryside. He slid from shadow to shadow, ducking low behind the intervening swells of land, trying to gain distance before the Comanche left their present business to look toward Three Oaks.

He ran hard when he found stretches of hard-baked dirt, where no dust would betray his footprints. He trailed a bit of brush behind him across anything that might show a track. He had no intention of being tied up with what was going to be discovered about Ray tomorrow, or perhaps the day after. The man had to be supplied with food somehow, and the supplier would soon know he wasn't picking up his rations.

His mind seemed to be going at full tilt. There were many side issues here. Anybody at the ranch might well suffer for Cobb's sins. That went for the boys, Bao, and himself, as well as Quita and José. He was going to have to warn somebody, that was for damn sure. And what about the town? Would Dry Wells fall victim to the anger of the old Indian?

He slipped into the window as silently as he had left. Removing his clothing, he hid shirt and pants, as well as moccasins, under a pile of blankets. As it was summer, he was sure they wouldn't be disturbed for a long time. He opened the door a crack and listened to the snores. He couldn't hear Palmer's alert breathing. Was the man awake?

If there was anything to that, he'd best get back into his dusty garb and slide out the window again. Better do that than chance being caught coming out of this room where he had no business being. He dressed again and went outside.

There was no sign, yet, of dawn in the eastern sky. He went

to the corral and sat on the top rail, wishing that Bao would wake up and start the cook fire. Coffee would taste really fine right about now.

He went into the corral and caught his horse. It wasn't the horse old Mule-Ear had been, but it was a nice roan gelding. He wiped the animal down with a handful of straw, talking softly to it all the time. When Palmer set his hand on Robert's shoulder, he almost jumped out of his skin.

"What're you doin' up so early?" asked the ramrod.

"Couldn't sleep. Sometimes I get like that. Then I go outside and find somethin' to do until folks wake up and make coffee. I sure wish Bao would **do** that."

"Did you hear somethin' a time ago...like coyotes, but not quite like? Way off. Almost out of hearin' entirely." Palmer's eyeballs glinted in the starlight.

Robert kept his voice steady. "Thought I did. Clear off toward the road to the east. I don't hear all that good, though. Might have been coyotes. Might have been the wind whistling round the shed."

Palmer grunted. Robert hoped devoutly that the answer had satisfied him, but he knew the man **was** thinking about Ray, out there among the swells all alone. Watching.

There was a sound at the back of the cook shed where Bao had his quarters. A clanking told Evans that the ash bucket was being emptied. Bao was up, ready to begin his day's work.

"Think I'll go see if I can help Bao with the fire," he said. "I need a cup of coffee real bad. You coming?"

Palmer grunted again. Then he said, "No, I'll get another few minutes of rest. We got a long day ahead of us today. Cobb wants us to ride the line to the north. He thinks we've had some stock slipping over onto Reddall's land."

"Not again," groaned Evans.

"No. Not this time. Reddall doesn't run stock any more. Not since this...gang...has been operating around here. This time it's safe as houses."

Palmer stalked off toward his bunk, while Robert ambled around the cook shed to meet Bao returning with the empty ash bucket. "Morning, Bao," he said.

The cook opened the door into the kitchen. "Come on in. I

got coffee ready for me. Can spare one for you, too. You up early."

Robert cocked his head, listening. There was no sound except for the mutter of flames rising from the stove, the hiss of wind around the building.

"I got troubles, Bao," he said.

"We all have troubles," said the Chinese, opening the door to fan the flames. "That no new thing."

"Worse ones, now. I wouldn't tell you before, but when Cobb asked me to kill the boys, I got him to agree to let me drive 'em crazy. Put 'em away in the crazy-house, then get himself made permanent custodian of the kids and the property." He gestured as Bao turned toward him, eyes fierce.

"I don't intend to do that, Bao. Just to put him off till I can find a way to make sure he can't get rid of 'em. But now something else has reared its ugly head. We got Injuns out there in the eastern hills."

The Chinese stopped in his tracks. "Comanche?" he asked, his tone carefully neutral.

"Comanche. Tall old fellow—lost his family a couple of years ago. Thought they killed him, but didn't. Bad mistake, there."

"How you know this?"

"Well...I went out last night to kill Ray. Found out I didn't have to take the trouble. This bunch already had him. He was the one singin' to the stars, before daylight. I saw him from pretty close up. That was one crazy hombre."

"Yes. Very crazy. Mean. Dangerous. Not like Indian, not like Chinaman, either. Try to rape Quita.. José horsewhip him. He lay for José ever since, but that old man, he one smart person. Tough, too. Ray never catch him off guard. José never where you think he be." Bao was mixing flapjacks, his hands busy, his gaze thoughtful.

"So old Buffalo Hump get Ray? Good. Some times there is justice."

"And now old Buffalo Hump is going to jump the rest of us, and I can't really think it will be justice if you and me and the boys and José and Quita get it in the neck for somethin' Ray and Palmer made happen."

56

Bao grinned. "Then tell. Not all. Just some. And as for boys...I think there is plan that will work." He leaned forward and began to speak in a whisper.

Robert felt his head reeling. He had thought that he was a con-man. This Chinese cook made him look like a piker.

CHAPTER TWELVE

"What the hell's the matter with those boys?" Cobb's harsh voice, just behind her, made Quita jump nervously. Anything did these days, since Ray had been found staked out on the range, his eyelids pinned open with thorns and his body done medium-rare.

She had been wondering the same thing, worrying as usual, but she tried to pass it off. "Everybody is acting strange, now. When Indians around, it time for be nervous."

"Don't tell me that. What they're doin' isn't just nervous, it's crazy. Jerkin' like somebody's got 'em tied up to strings. Makin' silly sounds, laughin' when there's not one damn thing to laugh about, these days. I've a mind to get Dr. Duncan out hereto see 'em. Damn if I ever seen two kids act that before."

"Why not let me take to town? They have not been there since their aunt died. Their cousin asks about them."

Quita felt sure her request was useless, but she made it anyway. She had the feeling that she ought to get the children clear of Three Oaks and turn them over to their kinswoman. Her father had been on the alert for the past few days, since finding the Indian sign left deliberately around the body of Ray Peters.

"No. They stay here. I don't want those idiots in Dry Wells tryin' to say I'm not treatin' them right and with them jerkin' and squawkin' and goin' on the way they are, that would be the first thing they'd think about."

"My father say Indian not go. Wait in hills. He think may be Buffalo Hump and his other sons. The ones Palmer did not kill, for they were not with the family two years ago."

Cobb turned toward her, his gaze fierce. "Who told you about that? That's not to be talked on, girl! All we done was to

get rid of some Comanche varmints and have a little fun doin'
it. They had no business on my land, anyway. I took care of 'em
and there's not one thing anybody can say about it. They're just
Injuns, after all."

"This not your land. The boys' parents give Indian right to
come and go as they always have done. They not know you in
charge. You murder them, and you torture them, too. If I Buffalo Hump, I would come after you. He out there, waiting. My
father say, and he always know."

Quita's tone was serene. Her hands were busy with skillet
and fork, as tender strips of sirloin moved from skillet to plate.
She was not afraid of Cobb, and he knew it. Her father had
made things plain.

Cobb caught her shoulder in a painful grip, whirling her
around to face him. His other hand was raised to strike her when
the skillet full of hot grease splashed full into his throat and
chest. The man screamed and released the girl.

"You go put cold water from well on that," she said, her
tone quite calm. "I finish with breakfast. You know keep hands
off me. My father will not like this, when I tell him."

Cobb didn't hear...he was streaking for the bucket of water
that always sat on the well-kerb outside the kitchen door. Behind her, Quita heard a quiet snicker.

"What are you two do?" she asked softly. "You try make
Cobb think you crazy?"

"Yes," breathed Andrew, as he limped to his place and
climbed into his chair. "Don't tell him, Quita. It's a *plot*."

"That man Evans, he say you do this?" she asked. Steak
joined eggs and hot biscuits on the thick brown plates before the
boys.

"He and Bao. They say to leave, Quita. You and José.
Leave soon. Those Indians are comin' back, they think. And
they're not going to care who was in on what happened two
years ago and who wasn't. They're prob'ly going to wipe out
everybody here. If they get Cobb, I don't care if they burn the
house down."

Kenneth reached to punch his brother's shoulder. Cobb was
returning, a streak of blister already forming across his thick
neck.

"I no trust Evans. Bao all right. Be careful," the girl whispered as she bent to fill two glasses with milk from the wild black cow she milked every evening.

Cobb was breathing heavily, his face russet with anger and pain. One glance at him silenced all conversation as the boys tucked into their breakfast, but Quita was not so easily quelled.

"You want me to go after the doctor?" she asked, as coolly as if nothing had happened.

Cobb's breath whistled through his nostrils. It was easy to see that he wanted to rise from his chair and throttle the young woman, but he controlled it. What José would do to him, should he manage such a thing, would make Ray's fate look pleasant.

"Might as well. Tomorrow's your reg'lar day. One day early won't hurt anything. Tell him I think somethin's wrong with both of 'em. He might take a look at Evans, while he's here. The man still limps more'n he ought, after so many days."

"Then I go this morning. Andrew, you cook dinner for me?"

Andy looked up at her and nodded. Then he made a strange sound, half laugh, half whinny. Cobb jerked at the sound.

"Damn if I know what's wrong. You tell Duncan to come tomorrow. I don't care who's having a baby or a broke leg. I want him out here."

There was never any temptation to linger over a meal under Jebediah Cobb's roof. The boys finished quickly, and Cobb didn't take much longer. Quita did up the dishes and put on her hat.

A trip to Dry Wells was just what she needed. The town needed to learn about the Indian affair. Minta must know about the strange behavior of her cousins, no matter if it was deliberate. Evans was an unknown quantity, and while the girl trusted Bao, she had no idea what the two were cooking up between them.

She had, as usual, her handgun, and this trip she kept it in her lap. That didn't help her at all when one of the Comanche rose from a mesquite bush she'd just passed and leaped silently into the back of the buggy. The first Quita knew of his arrival was the impact of his steely hand over her face.

Her breath was shut off, and she dropped the reins, trying

to pull them away so she could breathe. Something struck her on the temple, then, and she felt the world slip sideways.

Another blow sent her into blackness.

CHAPTER THIRTEEN

Everybody had been on the jump since Palmer rode in, three days ago, with Peters' body in a blanket. There had been no question about who did the deed...the Comanche had left plenty of sign, as if in warning to others an the ranch. Even Robert, knowing what it was that he would probably see, had been sickened by his brief glimpse of the swollen, staring corpse, with strips of charred flesh hanging loose from its banes.

The crew had ridden out the next morning to check the north line...but they were armed with extra weapons and ammunition, and four men circled their position, rifles cocked and ready far trouble. Palmer and Stinson bath *loo*ked rather pale and preoccupied, as did four or five of the other hands. Robert suspected that those were the ones who had taken part in the party two years before.

Some of Cobb's animals had strayed into the rough country north of the line, and Robert found himself alone among abrupt hills that were overgrown with cedar and oak scrub. The cow he'd chased into the tangle had a half-grown calf at her side, and he had to catch up to the group and get them back down with the cattle that were being held in a blind canyon. But he didn't like it. He kept recalling the look in the eyes of that old Indian.

The cow ran bawling into a thicket of bramble, followed faithfully by the yearling bull. Robert dismounted and took the rope from his saddle. It looked to be a long day.

The ground was rough and tended to sink into prairie-dog or gopher runs beneath his boots. He took his time, pushing his way into the stickery mess, running into prickly pear and thorny bushes along the way. He could see the end of a ratty cow-tail twitch, ahead of him. The cow thought she was hidden, because she couldn't see him. Cows had sense, but there were a lot of things they didn't know.

The Comanche dropped onto him just as he fell sideways, his heel sunk into a deep hole. The knife that had been intended for his throat missed him entirely, though the Indian was upright again with frightening speed. Robert, too, had rolled upright and was facing the warrior, his own knife in hand.

"Look," he said, "I don't want to kill you. I think you have a right to help your pa get his revenge. But I wasn't even here two years ago. You understand me?"

The black gaze flickered. The face showed no comprehension, but Robert was sure the man understood.

He didn't let that put him off his guard. He reached with his left hand for his pistol, watching the enigmatic face all the time. A twitch, so faint as to be almost invisible, touched the jaw line. Robert leaned aside and bashed the Indian behind the ear as he lunged past.

His knife was at the Comanche's throat when the black eyes opened. "We...will take...woman," said the man beneath him.

"What woman?" Robert thought of Minta Granger with sudden alarm.

"Mexican woman...from ranch. We will take."

Quita! He knew she was safely at the house...tomorrow was her day to go to town. But what if something took her out today? He had a sudden urge to find her and warn her.

He stepped back cautiously. He'd dropped his rope over the stub of a branch. He managed to get it loose without taking his eyes from his captive, and the Comanche wasn't stupid enough to try to jump him. The man watched contemptuously as Robert looped the rope about him.

"I'm tying you so you can get loose. You go and tell old Buffalo Hump that not all of us at Three Oaks are his enemies. Tell him to let the woman be...she has nothing to do with what happened to his family. Now I'm going. You get loose and go tell him what I said."

Robert gave a final jerk at the rope and stepped back. Then

he turned and ran down the slight slope toward his horse. He spurred the animal to a gallop, though over such rough ground that was dangerous. He didn't detour to find the crew...he had nothing definite to tell them except a strong hunch. They were scattered over the hills, working strays as he had been doing. If the Comanche he had caught had friends in the area they might find their own problems. That was their concern. He intended to warn Quita.

Robert had once seen a woman who had been captured by Apache. The memory left him shaken for years. She had hung herself later, he had heard, and he didn't blame her. Quita was a good woman, no nonsense or flirtatiousness about her. He didn't intend for her to suffer that fate if he could help it.

He rode toward the ranch, taking the easier route that required swinging to the east and coming in over the rolling hills near the road. The other way was more direct but would be much slower. He was hoping that he might find the elusive José, on watch somewhere in that area. He would be his socks that José could follow any track ever made.

Angling toward the private road, he tore across the rolling swells. After a time he caught a glimpse of something dark, ahead of him and to his right. He pulled his horse up and stared hard. A dark patch resolved itself into a man sitting on a big horse.

If it wasn't José, it ought to be. When Robert got nearer, the man raised his rifle, gesturing for him to stop. He waved urgently and kept going toward the waiting horseman. He spurred the horse to a gallop, and fortunately José didn't shoot.

As he approached, he knew with certainty that the waiting man was José. The stiff position on the huge bay could not belong to anyone else.

"They're goin' to try to get Quita!" he yelled, as he got within earshot. "Quita! A Comanche told me!"

José spurred his big bay to meet Robert and pulled up in a thunder of hooves and a swirl of dust as they came together. His dark face was expressionless, but the black eyes were kindling to anger. "Quita? How you know?"

"I caught me a Comanch' back in the hills over at Reddall's. I got him, and he told me they were goin' to get her. 'The woman at the ranch,' he said. If there's another woman at Three Oaks, I've never seen her. Thank God she goes to town tomorrow!"

José flinched. "She go today. I watch road, she pass in buggy a small time back. I think nothing...she sometime go for something Cobb wants."

They stared at each other for an instant before wheeling their horses and starting for the road.

"I have warn her not to go away from house, now. But she never think of danger on road...she has never know danger there."

They came to the track in a few minutes and each took one side, watching the ground with close attention. They followed it to the turnoff on to the main road, which was little better than a track. The narrow wheels of the buggy laid parallel lines in the dust...past a thick patch of mesquite...and there they were joined by three sets of moccasin tracks, running, widely spaced. There was a confusion in the road there, and the tracks veered wildly off into the dried grass of the range to the west.

They found the buggy hung up in another patch of mesquite. The horse was gone, of course.

And there was no sign of Quita.

Chapter Fourteen

José looked up at Robert, his black eyes glittering. Robert nodded toward the ranch. "Let's find out what goes on," he suggested.

"No." That was José. "I go after my child. Tracks go southwest, toward scrubland. I follow until I catch. They are not far ahead...look, the mesquite leaves have not yet withered on this broken twig. Go where you like. I find Quita."

Robert caught his breath. The old man would not allow his own internal pain to break through his guard, but this danger to his child had come very near to shattering his control. He turned the roan's head to follow Meléndez as the old man set out at a trot across the scanty grass, dodging between mesquite and chaparral.

The Comanche had not taken the trouble to hide their trail. That said that they either scorned the tracking abilities of their foes, or they were in too great a hurry to bother. At least, there were no traces of a pause for rape along the way.

I'm going soft, Robert thought, kneeing his pony between stickery masses of brush. *There was a time when I wouldn't of give a tinker's dam about what happened to a Mexican girl, Indians or no Indians.*

He reined in as José stopped his mount and dropped to the ground to study a confusion of horse tracks. Robert dismounted too, and looked closely. Four horses had joined the three they followed. The group had sat their beasts for a short time... probably arguing about where to go. Droppings were still moist, so it hadn't been long.

"José," he said, his tone rather hesitant, "we're right behind seven Comanche. I mean, they are right over the next rise,

66

maybe. And there's just the two of us. Don't you think we need to scout 'em, then go get help to get Quita away?"

"You do not know this land. I do," said Meléndez. "Over the next rise is a long drop to a loop in the creek that runs past the ranch house. Trees. Shade. Even a little water, even with the drought. They will go there for comfort as they ravish my daughter."

He stared at Robert, his gaze as fierce and wild as that of an eagle. "We will not give them time. I will not give them time. If you are afraid, then go. I ask no man to risk himself in my affairs."

He was checking the ammunition in the pouch tied to his saddle. His Winchester came out of the boot and he checked its load, as well. He had two Colts, and he loaded both, after working the action a time or two. When he was sure his weapons were ready, he drew the knife from his sheath and dug it sharply into his thumb. With his own blood, he drew a streak of scarlet down his forehead.

Robert had been checking his weapons carefully since the night he saw Ray taken captive. Now he watched José as the sick man turned to mount his big bay. Never had he seen anything more frightening, Robert thought. Not the necktie party at Tolliver's. Not the woman in Abilene, who had come within an inch of making a soprano of him.

If anything ever was made that could scare an Indian, it was José Meléndez at this moment. Robert mounted and followed him over the rise.

* * * * * * *

The scrub was thick and tall as it slanted down toward the creek. Bending low, the two men were able to keep their heads below the level of the growth. Not that it would fool a Comanche, Robert thought, but it made him, at least, feel a bit better about this hare-brained escapade.

Halfway down, José stopped and dropped softly from his horse. Robert followed suit, and he left the roan ground-hitched as José led off at an angle through a thick, prickly mass of dried growth. It was not only painful, it required painstaking care not to make a terrible racket while moving through it. José seemed capable of creeping with the skill of any Indian, as he approached the creek at a long angle. Robert, behind him, bled and cursed silently and felt each step out thoroughly before committing his weight to anything that might crack or crackle.

Before they reached their goal, they dropped to their bellies. Strangely enough, this was easier...jackrabbits and armadillos and other small animals evidently inhabited the mass, and they had minute trails tunneled beneath the tangle of upper trailers and branches.

Now Robert could see only José's boot soles, as the older man wriggled forward along the maze of intersecting passageways, forcing a way through for the width of his shoulders. He heard a roadrunner burst out ahead of them, and the two froze. The bird was a dead giveaway, if one of their prey should notice him. And Comanche noticed everything. Robert found himself praying hard that the skinny creature was heading deeper into the brush, rather than into a clearer space.

They waited, scarcely breathing, for several minutes. There was no sound other than the sigh of drought-stricken ground, the crickle of insects in the dead grasses, and the distant shrilling of a hawk. Robert had time to feel his lacerated knees, his punctured palms, his scratched and bleeding face. Everything stung with sweat, which poured harder as they no longer made any breeze of their own by moving.

At last José breathed a distant, "Now!" and they proceeded toward the trees they couldn't see. Either José had the instincts of a homing pigeon, or he knew the lay of the land incredibly well, Robert thought. Either way, they now made better time, moving out of the stickery growth into a smoother variety, studded here and there with yucca.

They hit the creek bank at a shallow spot where cattle came often to drink. Hoof prints and cow pats marked the edges of the trickle of water. No Indians were in sight. José flowed over the damp rocks like some strange leathery serpent and disappeared into the shadowy reaches upstream, hidden by more deeply cut banks. Robert swallowed hard. Then he moved after him, feeling as if an enemy was ready to drop squarely onto his back as he wriggled into the water on the other side of the clear place.

They moved as silently as minnows, keeping clear of the water when they could, setting their hands and knees with precise care. After a hundred yards of travel, José raised himself to peer out over the lip of the streambed. He jerked his head, and Robert stretched upward to look out, too.

A Comanche, looking inscrutable but indefinably bored, sat on a worn-looking block. His gaze swept the range to the east and north. He never looked toward the creek at all. Robert sighed softly and moved back into shelter. He was getting to know the patterns of José's boot soles all too well.

CHAPTER FIFTEEN

Quita was frightened, really frightened, for the first time in her life. She had come to, hands tied before her, draped over the back of a bony horse whose backbone had almost worked its way through her stomach before the Comanche paused and put her upright in front of the brave who had captured her.

She thought the thing that brought her to must have been the babble of talk when the group with her met the larger bunch that had evidently ridden down from some other dark deed. One thing kept her from giving way to hopelessness. Her father had been so emphatic about the danger while the Comanche were near that she had slid a long sharp hairpin into her bundled braids. It was like a rapier, almost, and she knew it was still in place. The pull of it against the loop of braid was distinctive, and it was still there.

She did not flinch as the rider behind pinched her breasts and punched her belly. She was thinking hard, and what he did with his hand at this moment was irrelevant. If she was lucky, one, at least, wouldn't live to tell about what was done to her, but she had to seem hysterical, while remaining completely cool and in control.

She realized very soon that the group was headed for the creek. This loop, some four miles below the ranch house, offered shade and water for men and horses. The bastards wanted their comfort while they raped and killed her. She felt her heart beat faster, her breath come hard. Firmly, she controlled her own reactions. Fear was her enemy, and it would kill her more surely than a Comanche knife.

The brave splashed his mount into the stream and pushed her off, laughing as she sprawled down into the wet gravel. She didn't mind at all. In the tumble, she managed to get her hand to hair and down again. The skewer-like pin was hidden in her sleeve.

When the man dragged her onto the bank, he flung her down again, hard enough to wind her this time. She rolled over, nevertheless, panting for air. When he came down on top of her, she had the pin ready. It went right through him.

It was a moment before his fellows, backed away to observe the fun, realized that she was on her feet and their comrade was not moving, except for a twitching of arms and legs. Two rushed her, on either side. Burdened by skirts, she did not try to run, but she met the one on her left with a fist in the nose, knocking him backward as the other bowled her over.

Three more joined the struggle, and it took them all to hold her down for long enough to secure her hands again. They were laughing, as if finding a white woman with the spunk to fight for her life was an unexpected pleasure. Whooping, they tumbled over her, striking her, clawing at her clothing until her long skirt and full blouse hung in strips.

One leaned over her, and she kicked savagely. He fell aside, clutching himself, and another, out of sight behind her, struck her hard across the back of the head. She refused to let it stun her. She wriggled like a snake, frustrating the hard hands and the lashing feet.

She thought she had gone mad when the shots rang out. Only when one of her attackers fell across her and she felt the heat of his blood soaking her did she realize that help had truly come. A fusillade rang through the cottonwoods, and the surviving Comanche, uncertain of how many attackers there might be, fled to their mounts and sped away toward the hills west of the creek. They left behind four of their number.

Quita struggled to heave the dead weight off her chest. Hands seized the dead man and hauled him away.

"You all right, Quita?" asked a familiar voice. She swiped at the blood in her eyes, trying to see. She found a piece of her ruined dress and wiped hard. It was Robert. She tried to smile.

When she looked beyond him, she saw her father, methodically scalping the dead Comanche she had skewered with her pin. "Papa!" she cried, "Why you do this thing?"

He didn't answer. He moved from the first to the second, working his way through the dead men until he had a set of four scalps like a grisly bouquet, held by their long black hair.

"I thought you felt that Buffalo Hump had a right to be angry and to attack us," she said. She found to her surprise that her voice was weak, and her knees threatened to let her down again when Robert pulled her to her feet.

"These are not Buffalo Hump's sons. They are drunkards and thieves. They follow better men than they, doing evil deeds and giving all their kind a bad name," José said. His tone was matter-of-fact. "I am giving them their due."

"Which you were in a fair way of doing when we butted in," said Robert. His hands were busy unbuttoning his sweaty shirt, which he offered to her with a flourish.

She looked down and nodded. What her dress covered wasn't much, and it certainly wasn't what a dress was intended to cover. The shirt would come in very handy.

"I will wash," she said, "if there is enough water in the big eddy downstream?"

"Women," said Robert, his tone disgusted. "Fight like a catamount, then worry about a little blood!"

"I worry about a lot of blood," she said quietly. "And I cannot bear the stink of them on me. I wash, or I stay here and walk home."

"Well, hell," he said. "Go down about twenty yards. There's a pretty good pool."

"Thank you," she said. "And thank you also for the shirt. It is appreciate."

She staggered away, around a bend, and tugged off the remnants of her clothing. She scrubbed for a long time before the sand and pebbles stung away the feel of greasy bodies and sticky blood from her skin. Only then did she don Robert's shirt and a sort of sarong made of a length of her skirt and return to face her father.

She could see, long before she reached him, that this had depleted his scanty supply of strength. He looked like a sick man no longer. Now he looked like a dead man.

CHAPTER SIXTEEN

Robert was relieved to find that Quita didn't take long to clean up. Time was important, now. When the escapees reported their failure to hold onto their captive, it was quite possible the rest of the Comanche, however many that might be, would try for someone else. And if they made the mistake of taking one of the boys, that would play right into the hands of Jebediah Cobb.

"I'm thinkin' about those kids," he said to José, as they watched the girl approach. "They've been told to stay close, but I know how they think. Those two live in their own world, and not much any grownup says to 'em soaks in very deep."

"You might be surprise," said Quita. She was wringing her long hair, from which water still dripped, as she came up beside him. "They do good job of being crazy for Cobb. This morning he tell me to get the doctor to see them. That is why I go to Dry Wells today."

"And they told you what was going on?" asked Robert, beginning to grin.

"Of course. They know I worry about them. They know I not tell their uncle. I hope to ask Duncan to take them away to his house, at least while Indians are here. You are clever man...what do you intend to do if they play-act so good they fool everyone?"

Robert shook his head. "I mainly want to get them away from Cobb. He wanted me to kill the two, when I first came. He wouldn't say it right out, but that was his intention. If they're safe, in the crazy-house, nobody can get at 'em until somethin's done about Cobb."

He helped the girl onto his horse; then he mounted the big

bay behind José. "I'd get 'em back out, when it was safe. Surely you believe that!"

She kicked the roan in the sides and turned her head toward the ranch. "I think you may do thing. But if something happen to you, what then? Think of those boys in with people who are really insane, perhaps for all their life. A terrible thing that would be."

Robert had, strangely, never thought of such an eventuality. Now, riding on the bay's rump, he found himself worrying about it. He had to get to Dr. Duncan; that was the next thing to do. When Quita and José were safely at the ranch, he had to take off for Dry Wells.

Could he persuade Cobb to let him take the boys with him? It was something to try, though he hadn't much hope of it. Cobb wanted those two right under his thumb. Or dead. That was the thing to remember...if he failed in his attempt to save them, someone else wouldn't cavil at shooting two youngsters.

They pounded up the track to the ranch and found Cobb on the porch, his rifle at the ready. At least, he wasn't taking the Comanche threat lightly. He might be a villain, but he wasn't a fool. His name had to be at the top of Buffalo Hump's list.

"What's all this?" shouted Cobb. "Where's my buggy?"

José stared down at him, his eyes hard as marbles in his ashen face. "The Comanche take my daughter; we only rescue her just before they ravish and kill her, and you ask about buggy? You are no man. You are animal!"

Cobb's face reddened. He tightened his grip on the gun... but Robert caught his eye and shook his head very slightly.

Quita had leaped from her horse and was making for the house, where she kept spare clothing. Kenneth met her at the door, and she put her arm about him as they went inside.

"That true?" asked Cobb. "They really got her, did they? I didn't think till she was out of sight that they might be keepin' an eye on the road."

Robert slid from the back of the bay. He walked to stand face to face with Cobb. "You thought about that, and then you sat here and let her go ahead, without going after her or sending somebody?"

Cobb's small eyes narrowed. "You don't take that tone

with me, boy. You work for me, remember ?"

Evans wanted badly to put his fist into the middle of the round face, but he held onto his temper with all his might. He could do that later, when the boys were safe. For now, he needed to have free access to the ranch. He found that he cared strongly about the fates of the boys and the Meléndezes.

He turned to help José over to the bench beside the wall. The old man was quivering. Not shaking, as with fear or chill, but quivering with the tension of a bowstring, his control almost at an end in its battle with the pain of the thing that was eating him alive.

Robert found himself aware, with sudden clarity, of the change in himself since he had come to Three Oaks Ranch. He had cared for nobody. Not even for himself. He had made no personal attachments, not even with Quita, though she was a comely woman and he liked her a lot. But now he found himself feeling responsible for four people. It was something he had never intended to do, yet the realization didn't trouble him.

Cobb was standing on the porch, his face inscrutable as he stared down at the two. "You awful chummy with that old devil all of a sudden," he said, his tone suspicious.

"This man is very sick," said Robert. "Or hadn't you noticed? He's dying, I think. It can't be more than a few weeks, now."

José seemed not to hear. He was withdrawn into some inner bastion, holding the pain at bay with an act of will. Anyone else, Robert thought, would probably have been screaming or writhing full-length on the ground. Not Meléndez. But he needed to be in his own house, in his own bed. The efforts of the morning had drained him dry.

Quita came out of the house again, dressed in one of her calico work dresses, a clean apron over its entire front. "Papa," she said, coming to stand beside José, "You must rest now. Come!"

She looked defiantly at Cobb, who had the grace to keep his mouth shut as she led her father away toward their small house, almost invisible beyond the cottonwoods. Robert stared after the pair, feeling suddenly at loose ends. There was so much to do, now, that the thought of deciding what came first

75

left him bewildered.

"Well, seeing as she didn't make it, you got to go to town after Duncan. Those boys're acting so crazy, I got to do somethin' about 'em." Cobb looked disturbed.

Robert, wondering what strange quirk the boys might have designed for the discomfort of their quasi-uncle, nodded. "What if I take 'em with me? With Injuns around this way, they'd be better off in town than way out here. The doctor could observe 'em for a week or so, just to make sure what's wrong. He probably couldn't tell, just from a short visit out here." He hoped his tone was properly neutral.

"Take 'em away? They're my responsibility," Cobb protested. "How can I look after 'em if they're off in Dry Wells?"

"But they'll be with the doctor. You can't be criticized for that," Evans said. "They seem to be sick...or disturbed. Anybody would say you've got to find out what's wrong. And as far as I can see, there's not but one way to do that. I had a cousin, once, who had fits. They had to send her off for six weeks to a hospital before they found out the poor kid wasn't crazy, she was just wormy!"

Cobb looked disgusted. But he seemed to be thinking about Robert's proposal. At last he looked up. "I guess so," he said. "Makes sense. And if the Injuns should get 'em, I'd never live it down."

He turned to yell into the house. "Ken! Andy! Get your things. You're goin' into town with Evans, here. At least till the Injun trouble dies down."

When he looked back at Robert, his small eyes were filled with something disturbing.

Robert felt a chill go down his back. Was it triumph? And in what way had he played into the man's hands?

CHAPTER SEVENTEEN

It had been over a year since Kenneth and his brother had left the ranch to go to town. Andy felt his heart thumping with excitement, as he packed his extra shirt, underwear, and socks. He never had but one pair of pants at a time, nowadays, and those usually were outgrown ones of Ken's.

When he looked up from strapping his roll together with the tooled leather belt his father had given him the Christmas before that fatal tornado, he found Ken staring at him.

"You reckon we need to keep actin' crazy?" asked the older boy. "It's kind of fun with Cobb, seeing him squirm, but Robert already knows we're fakin' it."

"We'll ask him, once we get clear of Cobb," said Andy. "I 'spect we can stop, once we're away from the ranch."

The two shouldered their light packs and went out to find Robert leading their horses, already saddled, up to the gate. "You all ready?" he asked.

Andrew rolled his eyes, let his mouth drool artistically, and spun on his heel. Ken just grunted dully, his eyes on the ground. He didn't enjoy the play-acting as much as his younger brother did.

"See that? See that? If those kids ain't crazy as bedbugs, I'll eat 'em both. If Duncan finds 'em crazy, it ought to be easy as pie to get 'em committed to the nuthatch." Cobb was looking smug again.

Robert knew he had visions of permanent custody of two deranged nephews, with the attendant free hand concerning Three Oaks that it would mean.

"Come on, fellows," he said, beckoning to the faltering pair. "I'll help you mount."

It appeared that Kenneth had forgotten which was his left foot. He mounted on his right and wound up facing the horse's rump. He could feel Andy restraining his laughter as he allowed Robert to put him right way around.

They headed up the track toward the main road, feeling Cobb's gaze chilling their backbones. However, once they were lost in the rolls of land beyond the ridge, Robert pulled up.

"All right, boys. You're doing a fine job with your uncle, but you don't have to fool me. I thought u the idea, remember?

"We turn off here. I expect that Buffalo Hump and his sons may still be watching this route. Those others weren't really a part of his group, just hangers-on, José said. So let's just mosey over yonder and stay clear of the regular trails."

Kenneth abandoned his act regretfully. Andy straightened up and sighed deeply.

"That's a relief. I swear, Robert, I almost got to thinking that Ken was really loco. He's good at it!"

They turned their horses' heads into the stretches of parched grass south of the trail. The ground was rough, grown with mesquite and sagebrush, but they made good time as they headed south, angling toward Dry Wells as accurately as Robert could calculate.

Kenneth, riding last, was enjoying the knowledge that this ride would not end up back in the vicinity of Cobb when a crack brought him up short. With horror, he saw Robert reel backward in his saddle and fall.

The roan spooked and ran, dragging Evans, whose foot had somehow caught in the stirrup.

"He'll be killed!" yelled Ken, spurring his own mount in pursuit. He was brought up short by four Comanche, who rode over a rise in the ground and barred his way.

Andy, who had also started after the runaway, had been caught as well. And only a trail of dust showed where their new friend was probably being dragged to death over stretches of stony soil, cactus, and sidewinders.

Ken found himself thinking harder than he ever had in his life. Without looking at Andy, he began to giggle, his voice shrill. He let spit drool down his chin and he crossed his eyes slightly. He hoped he looked as crazy as a coot.

Andy, just within his range of vision, fell off his horse and did a good job of having a fit. The Comanche, still on their horses, looked nonplussed. Then the old man gestured, and two of the young ones dropped to the ground and grabbed the boys.

Ken found that he didn't like being bound hand and foot, romantic as it might sound in a novel. The rawhide cut into his wrists and ankles, and every motion of the horse beneath him made it worse. Tied with his feet secured beneath the belly of the animal, his hands secured to the pommel of the saddle, he knew that any escape attempt he might manage would be useless. He'd never be able to ride properly to outrun the Comanche, and they knew it all too well.

Andy was cursing softly beside him, and Ken knew that he had been served similarly. So what did they do now?"

"Stay crazy," he whispered, hoping his brother would hear. He let out a maniacal giggle, just to keep the Indians off balance.

Andy gurgled deep in his throat and began talking in his made-up language. That had been a real stroke of genius, Ken thought, and the almost-comprehensible words had driven Cobb to distraction.

The old Indian rode up close and surveyed his captives. His aquiline face was stern and sad, and Kenneth remembered the reason he was there. Quita had made everything very plain to him and Andy, and he found his sympathies, unexpectedly, with the Indians, though he'd managed to hide that from everyone except Andy.

"Injuns ain't Christians," Andy had argued. "So they're no good to nobody and need to be killed off to make room for decent folks."

But the arguments hadn't convinced Kenneth, and he found, even in his present circumstances, that they still didn't. He stared wall-eyed at the old man and let foam drool from the corner of his mouth, nevertheless. He had no ambition to become an Indian, or to be skinned alive and gutted, the way Ray had been.

"You belong to Cobb," said the Comanche. "You will come with me."

The two young men caught the reins of both boys' horses

and led them over the rise after their father. They rode at a gallop for a long way, only pausing after crossing a stretch of shaley rock that would fool the best tracker ever born. At that point, they turned due north and rode into the grasslands that rose to the hills north of Three Oaks.

They had crossed the creek early on, and now Kenneth found himself in country he had never seen before. He tried to catch glimpses of landmarks, but one mesquite looks exactly like every other one. Even the patches of rocky soil were very similar. Only the sun, tracking down the western sky, gave him direction.

He could find his way home, when the time came. If the time came. Meanwhile, he giggled and drooled and looked as insane as he could manage, every time an Indian glanced back at him.

CHAPTER EIGHTEEN

Robert never did remember being hit. He came to lying flat, feeling as if he'd been run through a meat grinder, with his head a painful knob on top of his sore neck. He was flat on his face, staring eyeball-to-eyeball at a big ant, which was waving its antennae as if sizing up this humongous bit of food he'd found.

Robert snorted, blowing the ant away with a puff of grit, and heaved, trying to push himself up. His hands, he found, were battered almost beyond recognition and his arms felt as if they'd been pulled out of their sockets. It took him a long time to get himself into a sitting position, and even then he felt as if a hard breath would send his head after the ant.

He felt cautiously about his scalp and temples, though his fingers were all but numb. Grit and crusted blood covered him, and when he touched the crease left by the slug, he almost screamed. But he'd been lucky—the thing had only plowed a deep furrow along his scalp, instead of putting a neat hole into his skull.

Though every bone in his body was painful, he'd also been lucky that his boot stuck in the stirrup. If the roan hadn't carried him off, the Indians would have lifted his scalp. He glance down at his feet...the boot had evidently come off, leaving his right foot bare. Even the worn sock had gone.

The light was almost gone. He must have lain there for hours after falling free of the saddle. He was sitting in a small cup surrounded by stunted mesquites and prickly pear. He couldn't see the horizon. Only the dying light of the west showed him any direction.

"It's no good just sitting here," he said aloud. Something scuttered through the mesquite, frightened by his words. "I've got to get up from here and see if I can pick up a trail. Those boys have got to be in he hands of Buffalo Hump, and that's just what their uncle wanted."

He sighed. He didn't look forward to making the effort to rise. He had no idea if his feet and legs would even work...but the slither of a sidewinder down into the cup sent him erect without thinking twice.

He checked his belt. The knife was still in the sheath, but the worn leather of his holster was gone. So was the Colt.

"Damn!" He checked inside his ragged shirt. The little gambler's special that he carried for emergencies was still nestled under his armpit.

"Two by-God cartridges I've got to tackle a bunch of Comanche!" he exclaimed.

He looked down at his bare foot, whose toes were curling back away from the sharp grit and rock on which he stood. It was going to be a rough row to hoe, he had no doubt. Damn Cobb! If the man had been halfway decent, none of this would have happened at all.

Robert stared toward the west. The creek would be over there someplace. If he could make it that far, he'd clean up his wounds a bit, see if he could contrive some kind of covering for his foot, and then get some rest. As soon as it was light, he had to see if he could cut the tracks of the Comanche.

His legs held him up, which surprised him a bit. His right hip felt as if it had been wrenched loose entirely, but once he shook his foot back and forth a few times, it settled down to mere agony. His skin didn't bear thinking about. There was more of it strewn across the countryside than still clinging to him, he felt sure. Every time he moved, it felt that what was left was going to split and leave him bare as a spring locust.

He turned toward the last glimmer of light hanging over the western horizon and began hitching and halting his way along. He needed a walking stick, but the mesquites were too scrubby, not to mention stickery, to provide a branch long and straight enough.

He needed a crutch, to be honest. In fact, he needed an ambulance pulled by horses, not to mention a lot of water and some food. What he had was a body that still worked, after a fashion, and a destination. For the time being, that was enough.

The light sank into darkness. He focused on a clutch of stars and kept going. If he stopped now and let all his cuts, scrapes, and bruises stiffen up, he'd never move again, he knew. His head pounded a counterpoint to everything else, and he was relieved that it didn't start bleeding again with the movement.

It was his bare foot that gave him the most trouble. Every other step landed on something thorny or rough or sharp. He'd always had tender feet, even when he was a boy. Going barefoot in the summer never held any attraction for him. And now, when it would have helped to have tough feet, he was stuck with something that felt as if it had been ground up for sausage.

He plodded on, head down, gait that of a very sick old man. The line of dark shapes that were cottonwoods loomed up against the stars and drew nearer almost imperceptibly. Several times he had to stop, but he never sat or lay down. If he froze up, it was going to be standing up, headed toward his goal.

He reached the creek before daylight, which surprised him immensely. There was a puddle of water deep enough to sit in, and he plunked himself down into it and let the blood-warm ripples soak away some of the dirt, blood, and pain. He didn't touch his head...he knew scalp wounds, and he didn't want his to begin bleeding all over again. It didn't matter if he looked like death warmed over, if he could only get his feet and legs to working better.

Something stirred among the trees. He froze, staring into pitch darkness, as hooves moved toward him. Comanche... again?

He heard an inquiring whuffle of breath through equine nostrils. Unbelievingly, he said, "Roan?" as quietly as he could manage.

The hooves stopped. The horse snorted. Then it came on again and paused before leaning its dark-silhouetted head to drink from his bath water. He touched the nose, patted the forehead.

"By God, it's Roan!" he said. "Here, boy!"

He felt about the horse's neck and found a trailing strip of leather. The other rein lay over the saddle, and he pulled himself up to check what was left of his equipment. Rifle. Canteen.

Saddle-pack. Ammunition.

And moccasins! He almost cried with joy and relief as he staggered out of the water, holding to his horse, and dropped onto the ground, holding the reins in stiff hands that didn't relax their grip even when he dropped into sleep.

* * * * * * *

He woke feeling as if he was about to come apart at the seams. Everything he had, and some items he had never become acquainted with, sounded off with its own special twinge, ache, throb, or stab of misery. The sky was faintly light, and he knew he'd slept only a few hours. Yet there was no returning to unconsciousness. He had to get up...in one wild heave, if at all... and move.

He regarded a star, winking behind the dusty leaves of the cottonwood overhead. He felt down his legs and withdrew the consciousness quickly. Better not to think about it. Better just to do it and get it over with.

He heaved up onto his hands. His shoulders shrieked at him to stop, but he pushed on up, caught a nearby sapling and pulled himself upright. He hurt so badly that it canceled itself out. Nobody could keep track of all the pains, so he just turned his mind away and looked along the reins, still clutched in his left hand. The horse stared back at him, eyes glinting dimly in the darkness.

"Well, boy, we both made it. Now we've got to find those kids," he said aloud. His voice was a hoarse croak.

The horse whinnied softly in reply. Robert moved along its length, found the saddle...pushed far back by the drag of the day before. He loosed the girth, repositioned the saddle, and hauled himself up, using a handy low branch to help lift his weight. His left leg wasn't up to much, and his right was worse.

He groaned quietly, once he was settled. Then he clucked to Roan.

"Come on, boy!" He had drunk from the stream, but now he reached for the canteen and took a long swig from that, feeling the warm, brackish water slide down his abraded throat.

The sky was lighter. By the time he got out onto the plain,

it should be light enough to try tracking those Injuns.

He found out, all too soon, that those Injuns were not intending to be trailed...not by anybody at all.

CHAPTER NINETEEN

Robert found that having Roan didn't help him much, when it came to trying to track the Comanche ponies. He had to walk, crouched over, staring at every patch of dust or prickly-pear. The moccasins, however, were a great relief to his battered feet. As he tended to crouch, anyway, from the pain of his injuries, he covered a lot of ground before he finally quit his useless efforts and mounted the horse again.

"There's no way I'm goin' to find those boys this way," he observed aloud. Roan whiffled his nostrils and shivered his hide.

"I thought you'd feel that way," said Robert. "We're just goin' to have to out-think old Buffalo Hump. Where would I go, if I was an Injun with a couple of captives?"

He turned Roan's head westward, toward the creek. "I'd cross that damn creek. Then I'd head north toward the hills."

The roan whickered as he stepped into the shallows to cross the narrow stream. They turned north, keeping to the shelter of the trees but cutting off the deep loops that would have taken them far out of their way. They dashed across the brief spaces of exposure, feeling as if the Comanche nation might be staring at them from the reaches beyond them.

It had turned into a dust-hazed day, and high clouds puffed across the sky, hiding the sun often. They promised rain, but Robert knew it to be a bluff. It would not rain at this season of the year, unless it conjured up a storm of major proportions, and his weather-bone hadn't warned him of such a threat.

However, his bones were not in much shape to warn him of anything, being as full of aches and pains as if he were ninety instead of thirty. He found himself riding in a brown light that was turning purplish. Behind him, in the southwest, a line of black marked the approach of thunderclouds.

He halted Roan and stared back for a moment. Just what he needed...a ring-tailed buster of a storm to hide the trail even further. Then he came to his senses. He had no trail. If anything would or could hide his approach from the Comanche, providing of course that they had taken refuge in the hills, it was just such a storm as this one.

He rummaged in his pack and pulled out his poncho. He had enough troubles without getting soaked into the bargain.

He rode as quickly as he could bear toward the dusky tumble that marked the first line of gradually swelling hills. He began hearing the rumble of thunder behind him. Then, as he glanced back, he saw the lightning stitching from sky to earth and he saw the black billow...there was wind in that cloud, and a tornado was tearing toward him at the speed of an express train.

He dug his heels into Roan's side--on the good side--and the horse headed for the creek bed. They arrived in a downpour of rain, and he could hear the whining roar of the funnel cloud coming across the land, punctuated by bellows of thunder and now almost constant lightning.

They rode down into the overhang of the shallow banks, and Robert dropped, forgetting his pain, and pulled Roan's head around, forcing the horse to lie down in the shelter of the earth. He lay beside him, holding the beast's nose, fondling him, talking to him, though he couldn't even hear his own words now.

The world turned pitchy black. Even down behind the bank, they were covered with splinters of shattered mesquite, a hail of pebbles and grit. The rain washed it all off in runnels, and the cloud howled over and past.

The roar of the rain subsided to a steady deluge, and Robert crawled upright and let Roan rise to his feet. Already the stream was rising. He mounted, feeling every joint crack and groan, and headed the horse northward again. If Buffalo Hump was camped in this, he wasn't going to be expecting company.

Rain soaked through and around the poncho, down Robert's neck, and even his saddle was wet, irritating the insides of his thighs. His moccasins didn't protect his feet from the sudden chill following the storm, and he shivered from time to time as they plodded along the winding creek, going steadily north and east as the stream curved toward the distant spring that fed it.

As they neared the hills, Evans pulled closer to the trees. It was almost completely dark now, though the sun wasn't due to set for almost an hour. The cloud cover was thick and complete, however, and he found himself forced to depend on the stream to guide his direction. He had never crossed this part of the range before.

Roan was tiring too, and stumbled from time to time. At last, chilled and stiffening, Robert dismounted and walked beside the horse. When the rain stopped, he let the animal pause to graze a bit beside the creek. The grass might be tough with summer, but it was better than nothing. They moved better after that, and once they were well into the swelling curves of the hills, Robert stopped for the night. There was no way to find his quarry in the pitch dark in unfamiliar country.

He rolled in his blanket, which had dried from the heat of the horse's laboring body. Dropping into sleep like a pebble into a well, Robert found himself dreaming colorful dreams, knowing all the while that his head was pounding painfully.

The pain woke him at last. It was still dark, but the sky had cleared and Venus hung like a lantern above the east, where a line of light foretold dawn. Robert felt his teeth chattering. His face felt swollen and flushed, but his bones were cold.

He had a fever, he knew very well. Along with everything else! But he also had a job to do, and he groaned up onto his feet and staggered over to Roan, who was cropping dry grass and sighing as if bored.

It was almost more than Robert could do to heft the saddle onto the animal's back again. He had just slipped the bit, so that was easy, but cinching it tightly enough to keep the saddle from slipping around was a real pain. His muscles seemed to be without strength, his hands swollen so that it was hard to grip the girth.

After a bit he had things done and he chewed a bit of biscuit from his pack. All his teeth felt loose and sore, and the effort made his bullet-crease throb unmercifully. He had felt sorry for Buffalo Hump, in the beginning. He found that his sympathy had somehow melted away in the rain of the night before.

Now he was hurt, he was sick, and he was mad. Let the Comanche beware!

CHAPTER TWENTY

Many a time, Ken and his brother had slipped out of bed and through their window at night in order to go down to the bunkhouse and lurk under one of the windows. The hands told wonderful tales of shootings and sprees and Indians and outlaws. It had never occurred to Kenneth that at least a part of every narrative might be fiction.

He had always had a particularly soft spot in his heart for tales of capture by Indians. It seemed impossibly romantic and dramatic. He was finding that the stories he'd heard had been so exaggerated as to be pure damn lies. There wasn't a thing he could think of that was good about being the captive of Comanche, though he held out some hope that other tribes might be different.

He and Andy had made up stories of their own in which they were mountain men, captured and tortured, who made sudden and miraculous escapes. They had never thought in their wildest imaginings that as such captives they would be tied hand and foot to their horses, left unfed and unwatered, and ignored by those who had seemed so anxious to make their acquaintance.

Buffalo Hump had led the string of riders at a tremendous clip across the range, avoiding any patch of soil that might hold a track. Kenneth had discovered, by straining himself to twist and look back, that one of the younger Comanche had dropped far behind and scanned the ground over which the group traveled, obviously searching for any hint of a trace of their passing. Ken's heart dropped into his boots. How would Robert, if he was still alive, or José, if Robert was dead, ever find them now?

He was also shocked by the way the Indians treated their

horses. They simply rode them until they were ready to drop. When that happened, at last, they were well into the hills, amid a scruffy growth of mesquite and scrub oak.

Andy had been so exhausted by that time that Ken had to lift him from his horse. The bad leg was useless. The two sat and rubbed the knee and the calf until he had some control over the limb again. They were grateful that Buffalo Hump, seeming certain that they were too far from home to try escape, had released them from their bonds.

One of the younger braves passed, glanced at them indifferently and pitched a strip of jerky that was covered with dirt. Ken looked at the thing, which looked more like a bit of dead tree root than food. He felt his stomach grumble fitfully.

"I vote we eat it," he said to Andy, his voice as quiet as he could make it.

Andy looked at the thing with loathing. Then evidently he, too, consulted his belly. He got out his knife and cut the filthy strip into halves.

Ken scrubbed off all the dirt that could be removed against his pants-leg. Not that his pants were clean, but they were a darn sight cleaner than the jerky. He closed his eyes and bit at the meat. It was like trying to bite that dead tree root, the stuff being as hard as rock. There had to be a way to eat it.

He looked covertly toward the Indians, who were hunkered in a circle, grunting comments and chewing. He noted that they sucked at the jerky on its edges, nibbling away bits gradually. He tried it, and it worked. What was even more remarkable, the stuff was delicious.

It was late in the afternoon. The sky was clouding over rapidly, and Andy felt his bad leg twinge sharply, as if a storm might be over the horizon. He nudged Ken.

"I think we'd better take cover. My leg tells me we're goin' to get rain," he said.

Ken looked up. He sniffed the air, tested the direction of the wind. "Cyclone weather," he said. When Ken predicted a storm, it was time to get under a rock.

They moved cautiously past the group of Comanche, who were now playing a game on a buffalo hide that had been cross-hatched with white lines, something like a checkerboard. The men held handfuls of bits of bone, which they tossed onto the robe.

Although not one of the men looked up or seemed to notice that the boys were moving, he felt in his insides that Buffalo Hump was aware of everything as it happened. Maybe even before it happened. The thin old man had a hard edge to him...that was the best way Kenneth could find to put it. He seemed to cut right through everything, as if his purpose had grown so sharp with the passing of time that it had almost sliced through the man himself.

Andy tugged at his sleeve, and Ken followed into a cranny between two slabs of rock. A narrow end, just barely wide enough for the two of them, it was partly roofed, though at an angle, by another slab that had fallen from the small cliff fronting on the clearing where the Indians had stopped. The shelter was too small for a grown man. It was all but too small for Ken. But Andy fitted right into the notch, and Ken turned his back on the opening and decided he could protect himself pretty well from the rain if he covered up with his poncho.

They were tired from the long ride, and it wasn't surprising that they fell asleep almost at once. Kenneth woke to a horrendous roar. He clutched at Andy with both hands. He'd heard that before...and the tornado connected with it had killed both their parents.

Andy leaned forward and held Ken tightly in his arms. He hadn't forgotten that sound, either.

The world was black and filled with terrible noise. Their tiny space was filled with flying stuff that stung like bees, and Ken found that he could hardly get his breath. The zooming roar moved past... it had not gone over the camp, he thought, though it hadn't missed it by much...and the downpour of rain seemed quiet by contrast.

"You suppose it got the Injuns?" asked Andy.

He shook his head. "They know how to get by if anybody does. I'll bet they're out there right now, gettin' things back together."

There was no use in going to see. Buffalo Hump had built no fire, and now it was dark as midnight. The boys huddled as close as possible, trying to warm their wet bodies. Ken wanted to cry, but he refused to let Andy know, and they were too close to hide such a thing. They slept by fits and starts, and when the first light crept into the crack where they had sheltered they crawled out gratefully. Even Indians were better than a tornado.

The horses were there. All the Indians, too. Ken had known they would be. They'd lived in this country a lot longer than the whites had, and they knew how to survive almost anything it could throw at them.

They were crouched around a tiny smudge of fire, quiet, chewing on jerky. Ken and Andy approached hesitantly. Again, the young Comanche tossed a strip of jerky. This time the boys showed no hesitation about eating it.

They had finished that, and the Comanche were having some sort of discussion when Ken glanced up to see what had startled a roadrunner from the mesquite. Something was moving through the brush.

Buffalo Hump said something, his tone sharp. The other three slid to either side, leaving their father to face the bloody, frightening figure that crashed out of the mesquite and faced them, rifle at the ready.

Ken gave a stifled gasp. He'd never seen anything so terrible in his life—it was like a scarecrow that was altogether too much like a man for comfort. The clothing was in shreds. The skin showed great red patches of rawness, and he thought he could even see glints of bone as it moved.

Buffalo Hump stood quietly, as the rifle came up.

A familiar voice said, "I've come for those boys. You better not give me no lip, either. I'm just about out of patience."

"Robert!" shouted Kenneth, and his brother echoed the cry.

CHAPTER TWENTY-ONE

By the time he smelled the faint tang of smoke from the Comanches' tiny fire, Robert was almost reeling. His body was too painful to think about, and his head was swimming with fever. He alternately shivered and sweated, as he led Roan through the scrubby growth, following his nose as best he could.

The sky grew lighter, and he saw, off to his right and ahead, a jut of stone against the light drift of cloud that was becoming pink as the sun came into view. When he staggered toward it, the smoke-smell was stronger. Even the Comanch', he thought, needed the comfort of a fire after such a wild night.

He checked the load of his rifle. Its weight was torture to his battered hands, and it was impossible to crook it in his arm. There was no skin there to keep it from resting on bare nerves. He held the weapon before him, ready for instant use. Before he got too close, he looped Roan's reins about a mesquite. Then he trudged forward, setting one foot before the other with concentration. His moccasins were silent on the soaked ground, and fallen leaves and twigs that would otherwise have crackled were too wet to make a noise.

The roadrunner that fled before him startled him. That would have warned the Comanche too. He stumbled through the scrub into a small clearing and stared, rifle ready, at the huddle of Indians who slowly broke up into a line centered by the man he had seen supervising the end of Ray Peters.

He was conscious that the boys had yelled, but it took everything he had to keep his mind focused on what he was doing

"I come for the boys," he said. He was surprised that his voice would come out at all, even as a harsh croak. He cleared

94

his throat. "They had nothin' to do with your folks. You want their uncle. He's the one that made all your trouble. These boys, they're suffering from that man, every day of their lives. He got me out here to kill 'em, but I wouldn't." He felt himself swaying, and Robert knew he was talking too much.

The old Indian was surveying him intently. The black eyes, almost hidden in the deep folds of eyelids, seemed to pierce right through him. But a recklessness had hold of him now, and Robert felt compelled to say what was on his mind.

"You don't want to bother Quita or her pa, either. They're just about the only decent folks on Three Oaks Ranch. Oh, and Bao, the cook. He's a good little fellow, too. But you kin do what you like with Cobb. Spit him over a slow fire. String him up to a mesquite and pull out his guts. I don' care...." Robert felt himself swaying worse than ever. His eyes seemed filmed, and the group of Comanche was hazy now.

He felt a small hand catch his elbow. A larger hand caught his other side, helping him to stand straight and still.

"These're good boys," he said, his tone deeply serious. "Can't let you hurt 'em...," and then he couldn't say another word.

Held up between Kenneth and Andrew, he saw the Comanche approach him, staring and staring as if to winnow out the secrets of his soul. The grizzled head nodded once, sharply. A lean hand came out to touch his rifle, taking it smoothly from his grip. There was some reason why that had to be a bad idea, but he lost the train of thought and then it was too late.

He could, however, still hear, still see, though dimly. When Buffalo Hump spoke, he was aware of the old man's words.

"I know a warrior when I see him," said the voice, as if in a dream. "A man who comes, as you have done, when his body cries out against it, who speaks his heart when he burns with fever, is one I will listen to. My own heart is sore. I am angry with years of stored anger. My women and my children were killed without mercy and without even a chance to defend themselves.

"I am not such a one as Cobb. If he will not suffer to lose these young ones, then it is no revenge to make them suffer. Take them and go."

But it was the boys who took Robert. As Buffalo Hump's generosity did not extend to releasing the boys' horses, they had to support him on either side, as he came and went. He did manage to tell them that his horse was tied beyond the thicket, which helped the pair a lot.

They got him onto Roan with a great deal of difficulty. Just as they had gotten it through his head that he needed to help them heave him upward, he would slip away into a fevered dream and relax, sliding through their hands to sit on the ground. Ken's size and strength saved the day...he lifted Robert and hung him over the saddle, stomach down, as if he were a corpse.

Even then, Robert came to from time to time, staring beneath Roan's belly at a world upside down. It puzzled him a lot, but he always went away again into a cottony darkness that cushioned the worst of the pain of the motion.

It seemed to take forever to get wherever the boys were taking him. It grew dark, and they stopped and built a small fire of dried mesquite and cow dung, but then it was light again, before Robert was used to lying flat instead of swaying along, head-down.

Every nerve he had was lined with fire, and his head pounded with every step Roan took. When they stopped, at last, in the shade of the cottonwoods, he was too far gone to realize that they were near the ranch-house at Three Oaks. He didn't hear Ken slip away toward Quita's small cottage, and he didn't know when Andrew awkwardly washed his terrible face with a wet corner of his shirt-tail.

CHAPTER TWENTY-TWO

As soon as Robert and the boys were out of sight, Quita left the ranch house and went to her own cottage. Her father was abed, silent, unmoving. She knew he was controlling his pain with all the force of his dreadful will. There was nothing she could do to help him, but she couldn't bear to leave him completely alone.

When Cobb had called after her, she had ignored him. She and José had lifetime tenure here, and nothing Cobb could do would send them away. She had talked at length with the lawyer about that, and he was keeping a quiet eye on activities at Three Oaks Ranch.

The night had been long, black, and violent. She heard wind beyond the pounding of the rain, and she hoped Robert and the boys had stayed the night with Doctor Duncan in his well-built home. She had risen from time to time and stood beside José's bed, bent to hear his faint breathing. Once she had touched his wrist, for the noise of the storm was so intense that there was no hearing him at all.

When dawn came at last, she felt dragged-out and sore, as if she had spent the hours of darkness outside in the tumult of the weather. She made a thin mush and fed it to her father, who ate with determination.

He looked up at her, as he swallowed the last spoonful. "I will live a while longer," he said. "Those *niños*...they need me still. You go now. *Soy bueno*."

She managed to work about the cottage for a time, using the excuse that the rain had settled the dust, so she could sweep and dust to some advantage. By the time he was sleeping again, she had run out of things to do. Reluctantly, she changed to her working blouse and skirt, with the big apron, and went onto her pocket handkerchief porch.

The sun was brilliant in the freshly washed sky. The cottonwoods gleamed, the laundered leaves shining on the upper sides. The air smelled wonderful, with hints of mesquite and sage and clean earth moving on the light breeze.

It seemed a shame to waste such a day cooking and cleaning for such a man as Cobb. She sighed and went down the steps. But it was almost noon, and she had to fix his lunch or he would be even nastier than usual.

Something moved toward the creek, and she turned to stare in that direction. Putting her hand over her eyes .to cut down the glare, she saw someone running toward her. A familiar shape... Kenneth. Her heart thudded suddenly against her ribs.

He was supposed to be in Dry Wells with Doctor Duncan! Why was he running toward her from the creek?

She lifted her skirts and ran to meet him, and as she drew near she saw that he was terribly dirty, his clothing snagged and torn, his eyes wild in his grimy face.

"Kenneth!" she shouted. *"¿Qué pasa?"*

"Comanche!"

She turned cold as she stopped to face the boy.

"Got Andy and me. Shot Robert. Took us to the hills."

"Come!" He reached to catch her hand and tug her toward the cottonwoods.

They arrived in the cool green shade to find Andy kneeling beside Robert, who was lying flat on the damp sand of the creek bank. The water, high because of the rain in the night, was muttering very near to his out flung hand.

She was appalled at the man's condition. Rags of skin, flaps of torn clothing, punctures and abrasions...his body was a mass of injuries. She tore off a length of petticoat and plunged the cotton cloth into the gritty water.

She carefully sponged the worst of the spots on his scalp, but she was filled with curiosity. "How do you find him? How do you get away from the Comanche?"

"We didn't find him. He came after us and took us away from old Buffalo Hump," Ken piped up. "Scared us most to death when he come bustin' out of the mesquite, all bloody and tore up. Sort of scared the Comanche, too, I think."

She glanced up, startled. "A man hurt so, he could not follow after Indios," she said. *"¿Es verdad?"*

Ken touched her shoulder. "It's true. Robert followed. Caught up. Talked to Buff'lo Hump. Got us free. Then he folded."

Quita was unused to hearing so many words from the taciturn boy, but she had never doubted anything he said, scanty though it might sometimes be. Andy had an active imagination, but Ken stated facts.

Robert groaned as she compressed the damp cloth against a long groove in his scalp. The bullet furrow, she thought. She turned him carefully, getting the boys to help, and when she saw the rest of him, she knew she had to get him into the house. This was going to take more care than could be offered on any creek bank.

"Go after Bao," she said to Ken. "Take care. Do not let Cobb see."

The crew had left for the day. Bao would not be busy cooking until mid-afternoon. She hoped he would hurry, for this was a task so huge that she didn't know where to begin.

"Tell him...bring medicines!" she shouted after the boy. "He have some good ones."

She didn't try to do much more than keep the flies away while she and Andrew waited. She was thinking, now, of something else.

"Your uncle, he does not know you are return. Do not let him see. We keep you in the little house, where you will be safe. You think?"

The boy nodded. "We don't want him to get his hands on us again," he agreed. "But with Robert there, hurt, won't he come to see about him?"

She looked thoughtful. "You have secret place, eh? Where I never find you. I know. So you go there. Camp out until we see what is best to do. How you think of that?"

"Sounds good to me. We can pop back and forth to see about Robert, too. You think it's a good idea even to let Cobb know he's back?"

Their eyes met. Quita saw the same thought in the boy that

she was beginning to have.

"No," she said. "I care for him in little house. I go often to see to my father. Nobody think it strange to see me go back and forth. We keep him secret. At least...until Robert is able to defend himself again. Is good plan."

She looked up as leaves rustled up-creek. Bao and Ken were slipping along in the shelter of the cottonwoods. They too had the same thought. Cobb might not like to allow Robert to live now.

CHAPTER TWENTY-THREE

Robert came up from a well of fevered unconsciousness, trailing behind him a cloud of worry. It took him a while, once he was able to open his eyes, to pin down exactly what all he was worried about. Quita's face, hovering over him, distracted his attention.

Then the symphony of miseries hit him, and he groaned.

The girl frowned. "You be still, now. I have you clean up. Bao will tend you while I go to cook for Cobb. Nobody must know you here. Cobb think you are in town with the boys, and he must not find they are here, too."

"How'd I get here?" he croaked.

She smiled, though her forehead was still creased by a worried frown. "The boys. They brought you in. Quite a thing for crazy boys, you think?"

He tried to chuckle, but she touched his forehead with a damp cloth, and pain sent his thoughts scattering like a covey of quail. But he managed to stifle his moans, as she smoothed some sort of aromatic salve onto his battered skin.

An apologetic cough from someplace interrupted her. She turned toward a door...must be José's room, Robert thought... and disappeared from is line of sight. He heard mutters of talk, another cough that was almost a groan. José must be a lot worse now, he thought.

When Quita returned, she came to the side of the cot on which Robert was lying. "My father knows all the boys could tell me. If you feel well enough, maybe you tell him what happen to you? I must go. Cobb must not come here."

Robert heard her go, but his head was reeling gently, making the world rock and the walls slip around in odd configurations. Yet he knew now what was fretting his mind.

"José," he called softly. "Can you hear me?"

"Sí," came the quiet reply from beyond the wall.

"Buffalo Hump is goin' to come. He wants Cobb, and he wants the men who rode with Cobb and killed his folks. He turned the boys loose—I think I recall that and didn't dream it. We've got to get Quita and Bao and the boys away from here. Can you think of anything that might work?"

"My friend, I have reach the end of my rope. I cannot rise from this bed. It shames me to say it." José's voice was weary beyond belief.

Robert suspected that anyone less tough and determined would have been bedfast for months. "No sweat. No sweat. I'll just have to figure something out, that's all. There's something else, though. When I was lost—not that Cobb was worried about that, of course—I was with Hi Tolliver's bunch. What I told was partly true. But it was mostly a lie—I agreed to work with Tolliver to catch Cobb in the act of rustling. Now, with all the Indian trouble, I won't be able to do that, I'm afraid."

"Why does it worry you?" asked José. "You are now free. Tolliver cannot reach you here, for not even Cobb knows."

Robert felt shocked. "I gave my word!" he protested.

José began to chuckle. Then he fell silent, and Robert knew the motion had brought on an attack of pain. After a long while, José spoke again.

"You are terrible crook, Robert Evans. Worry about two boys you hardly know. Worry about giving your word to a man who would hang you. Worry about Chinese cook and Quita. Such *hombre malvado* I have never see!" He coughed softly.

"I am die ver' soon. I am old, and the old have no conscience, so I give you more worry. You take care of my Quita. She good woman, strong and brave. You no marry her—I see that. But you will take care while danger is here. After that, she take care of herself ver' well."

Robert felt all his aches and pains descend on him at once. For a man who had spent most of his life running from responsibility, he was getting more than his share now. And the worst thing about it was the fact that he knew he wouldn't run. Not this time.

102

There came a fumbling at the door. "Is Bao," came a soft voice. Bao's round face peered around the doorframe. "How you feel, José?" he asked loudly.

Robert knew it was for the benefit of anyone keeping an eye on the Meléndez house.

José croaked a reply, and the little cook came into the room and pushed the door halfway shut. A fitful breeze stirred the hot, dry air of the room, and Robert was grateful for that.

Bao went into José's room for a while. Robert took the opportunity to doze, and when the Chinaman returned, he was clearer-headed than he had been.

"We've got to warn the people at Dry Wells that there are Injuns up here," he said. "Buffalo Hump may quit when he gets what he wants, but I'm not too sure about his sons. They looked pretty wild to me."

Bao smiled, his cheeks creasing deeply. "Cobb left for town pretty-soon this morning. He say he check on boys, talk with doctor, make sure people know he is concerned. He will find that you and boys did not arrive. Then he make a lot of noise, say he will go find you all and save from Indians. He will come home and smile."

Robert found himself laughing, though it hurt like hell. Bao had assessed the situation accurately, he was sure. There was noting that could suit Cobb more than having his nephews in the hands of Indians. Even if he found them, he could kill them and say he found them dead, and nobody would ever be the wiser.

"We've got to get those boys to a safe place," he said when he sobered. "I expect the Comanche just about any time now. Cobb may think he has enough men here to keep them off, but he doesn't know Buffalo Hump. That old man would tackle Hell with a flint knife, the mood he's in. And he just might come out on top. I have the feeling he's got more men stashed up in those hills, too. There will be more than the four of them, I'd bet on it. Is there any way we can get those boys away?"

"Boys hidden good," said Bao. "We must get you and José away. Quita worry. I worry. We all need hiding place. I find boys, they tell me how to get to their place. Then we all go there." He sighed. "Mebbeso, it is too small. Could be we will have no time. But will see."

Robert held up a hand. "Here, give me a heave. Let's see if I can stand on my feet. I don't think anything vital is broke."

Bao tugged at his hand, and he managed to sit, though the remaining skin on his body protested loudly. Robert put his feet over the edge of the cot and touched his battered soles to the floor. It hurt, but he kept on, holding onto Bao.

He managed to stand at last. It was, if nothing else, a beginning.

CHAPTER TWENTY-FOUR

Buffalo Hump had carried a hard, hot coal of rage inside his breast for two years. The loss of his family had gone hard with him, but the loss of his dignity at the hands of Cobb and his men rankled even more deeply.

He had set himself to healing his body as quickly as possible, though at his age it had taken a bit longer than it had when he was a young man. He had, as soon as he was able, run for miles every morning. He had overcome the broken bones, the shattered hand, the foot that seemed, for a time, to refuse to heal properly.

His younger wife had helped him greatly, feeding him well, encouraging him to greater and greater efforts. His older wife had been her friend from childhood, and they had lived as sisters in his home. His sons had gathered to his side, though it meant neglecting their own families and hunts and responsibilities to their branches of the tribe.

Once he was ready to take the war trail, many other young men were anxious to join him. It had been too long since they had known the opportunity to raid the whites, to ravish their women, and to entertain their men with torture and death. Some of those young men were warriors, and he was happy to have them at his side. Many were idlers, grown weak and vicious, eating the white men's meat and letting their strength run away like water.

He let those come, too. He needed as many members with his band as he could find, for he intended to wipe the hunting trail clean of any trace of Three Oaks Ranch and its inhabitants. If they entertained themselves at the expense of other whites than those he intended to kill, that was their business. He had lost his patience with the entire race of pale-eyed people.

The encounter with the watchman in the grasslands had been uninformative. That had been one of those he had met two years before, of course, and the fact gave some solace to Buffalo Hump's wounded spirit. Full measure of repayment had been exacted from the man. He had died like a warrior, full of defiance to the end, which made his death more satisfying..

Yet after that it seemed that he had lost some measure of control over those who followed him. Only his sons and his nephews did as he asked them, keeping watch over the road and the ranch. Some of the others went their own ways, and those who had seized the woman had paid dearly for their short-lived pleasure.

Buffalo Hump gathered as many of his following as he could call together and pointed out the disaster that had overtaken that rash band. "I am here for a purpose," he told those who were not of his blood. "You may do as you wish, as long as you do not interfere with my vengeance. But if you make trouble that brings many men against us, so that I cannot destroy those who killed my family and dishonored me, then I will turn my hand against you, as well.

"Hunters do not frighten away the game of other hunters from the same tribe. Hold that in your memories. The game I seek is two-legged, but that is the only difference." He glared about at the assembled group.

"The grassland runs with beef. Feast and enjoy yourselves. But do not interfere with my purpose. I will tell you when it is time to go against those at the ranch. I want them to live in fear for many days, to look to the horizon for the shapes of warriors, to lie down to their sleep with their skins crawling with apprehension. Do you understand me?"

"Uh!" came the reply from the men...all of them. Buffalo Hump, it was widely known, did not make idle threats.

His sons nodded gravely. They were a handsome lot, ranging in age from the mid-forties to late teens. His wives had given him many sons, and his sisters, too, had borne man-children.

When the group split up again, the rebellious ones were sobered and more cooperative. They rode off to wait in the hills for his signal, while he divided his sons and nephews into four groups and sent them to watch, again, the roads, the ranch, and the town, while he roamed between them, keeping his eye alert for any opportunity for harassment.

The chance to seize the children was too good to miss. He had thought, when the man fell and was dragged away, that he must be dead. Yet Buffalo Hump had lived too long to take any chance. He headed at once toward the hills, knowing that he could conceal his captives there for as long as he needed.

The weather had not troubled him. His purpose burned so hot inside him that he knew not even the gods of wind and lightning and thunder could interfere with it. And so it had proved...the tornado had gone a good eighth of a mile to one side of his camp. The rain had merely dampened him without cooling his fury.

It was the arrival of the man that had shaken him.

Buffalo Hump knew a man and a warrior when he saw one. This was one who drew upon inner strengths that few possessed. That was plain when he walked into the camp and demanded the boys. Such determination was a rare thing in red or white, and the old chief found it impossible to refuse him.

Yet once the captives were gone, Buffalo Hump found himself confused. His focus of purpose seemed to have faded a bit, leaving him undecided what to do next. He knew it was time to go into the hills and seek for a vision, though he hesitated to leave his bands without leadership, even for a day.

At last he called those of his people who were with him at that last camp together. "Gather all our people together," he told them. "Go into the grasslands to the west of the creek and hunt for beef. Eat and grow strong, while I seek for a sign. In three days, come to this place, and I will be here."

He turned at once and mounted his horse. He did not look back to see if they obeyed him. He knew his sons and his nephews. They would control those others. Except for some cattle, nobody would suffer for three days.

After that...then the suffering would truly begin.

CHAPTER TWENTY-FIVE

Three-Coyotes-Howling-at-the-Moon was hungry for meat. He was hungry for blood. He was not a man used to taking orders, as were, indeed, all his fellows. When told to go and hunt in the grasslands, letting the fat rancho, with its many buildings and resident woman, go unmolested, he turned his face toward the hilly pasturelands. If Buffalo Hump wanted him to hunt, then he would hunt with a vengeance!

He found that without the subduing effect of the kinsmen of Buffalo Hump among them, the group was easy to rouse to mischief.

"We will go among the herds in those grassy places, and we will drive many of them into the hills, where we will eat meat until fresh blood drips from our elbows," he said.

He found an enthusiastic response. After a night or rest near the branching of a creek, he rode out in a dry dawn, followed by six others. The wind was sweeping across the land, rather gently on this morning, and raucous birds were calling from the scrub-oak as the small band loped down a slope and across a broad sweep of grassland.

The rains had brought out green among the tan stalks. At a distance, Three-Coyotes could see small clusters of cattle, heads down, grazing while the day was still relatively cool. He headed for the hillside on his right, and without a word spoken three of his companions followed while the other three moved wide to approach the herd from the other side. Driving cattle was not much different from driving buffalo, and they were expert at that.

Three-Coyotes crossed the hill and swung around to come at the animals from behind. When he was in position, he kneed his horse into a gallop, at the same time letting out a shattering wail.

"Y-i-i-i-i-i!" he shrieked.

The nearest cows flung up their heads, eyes rolled back in frantic terror. The older of the two bulls grumbled deeply and turned to face the enemy of his herd, while the younger led the cows away from the approaching riders.

Ignoring him, the Comanche avoided his rush and lit out after the rest of the cattle. Yelps in the distance told Three-Coyotes that his fellows were keeping the rest of the animals moving. He kicked his horse in the ribs and galloped forward, turning a rebellious cow back to go with the rest.

They drove the animals hard, taking them up the long narrow valley and back over the gentle hills toward the more heavily treed country in which they had their camp. The tracks they left behind them were mingled and mixed. Only another Comanche could have unraveled the hoof prints of unshod ponies from the jumble of cattle tracks.

They knew exactly where they were going, of course. Three-Coyotes had spotted a draw with steep sides and an easily barricaded entrance, and into this they took Hiram Tolliver's cows and his best young bull. Only when the beasts were secured behind a brush barrier did Three-Coyotes turn back along the way he had come.

When the Comanche were done with their work, not even another of their own kind could have tracked Tolliver's lost herd to its hiding place. Three-Coyotes was a master at the game of concealing a trail. He knew that the feasting that night would be perfectly safe from any intrusion, and he built the fire himself.

When Buffalo Hump's sons returned to the camp, after making certain that the whites were settled for the night, they were not at all dismayed to find fresh beef roasting over the fire. It was as Three-Coyotes had said—they ate until blood and meat-juices dripped from their elbows.

The animals, of course, were bawling and butting and trampling in the draw, trying to find a way out. There was little water there and no grass for such a number of cattle. The Comanche, however, were not concerned. They would, if they remained for long, eat all they could and drive the rest back home with them.

Three-Coyotes was filled with triumph. If he could not strike at the whites on the rancho, he could still make trouble, which was his favorite pastime. He didn't truly imagine, however, the extent of the result his reckless raid would cause.

CHAPTER TWENTY-SIX

It had seemed like such an exciting thing to do. Andy had wanted for a long time to camp out in the hiding place he and Ken had found beneath the creek bank. He'd known, of course, that it was most unlikely that his uncle would ever let them remain unaccounted for long enough to do such a thing, so it had gathered all the glamour of the unattainable.

Now, forced to do the thing he had wanted so badly, he found that the ground was damp and the pebbles ground into his hide, however he squirmed to find a comfortable position. He would sweep away the ones that bothered him most, only to find that others took their places at once.

"You asleep?" he asked at last, his tone quiet in case Ken was actually finding it possible to rest.

There came a grunt and a snuffle. "Nope," said his brother. "Never thought it would be so miserable."

Andy knew exactly what he meant. It was just like being captured by Indians. It might seem like a good idea good idea when you read about it in a book or daydreamed about it in comfort but the reality left a lot to be desired.

He squirmed again, onto his stomach, and put his chin in his hands. The creek murmured along, invisible in the darkness, and leaves on the cottonwood and scrub-oaks fluttered faintly in the never-ending breeze. He sighed heavily. He'd never thought he could possibly long for his bed in a house with his uncle, but he did. The feather mattress seemed like a distant dream, beautiful and out of reach.

A new note joined the voices of leaves and water. A thudding, quiet and almost stealthy, moved along beyond the creek. Andy reached to touch his brother's shoulder.

"Ungh!" came the quiet grunt. Ken slithered away from his hand, and Andy knew he was moving across the water to see if he could catch shapes silhouetted against the stars.

Andy lay still, biting his knuckles to keep his teeth from chattering. Some hero he had turned out to be, he thought. Scared to death by the sound of hooves in the night.

Then he remembered the Indians. He hoped Ken had thought of that, too...it would be worse than bad luck to be captured twice so close together. And this time Robert wasn't up to coming after them, even if he knew where they were.

He could hear his heart thumping almost as loudly as the hoof beats. He hoped the Indians couldn't hear it, too. He breathed deeply, as Robert had taught him, and it helped him to relax a bit. The sound of a pebble grating against another undid all his good work, however. He went still as a hunted rabbit in a thicket. "Ken?" he breathed.

"Uh-huh." That was another breath, almost inaudible even at close range. His brother slid back beneath the overhang and curled against him. Andy could feel him shaking with tension. He opened his mouth to ask questions, but Ken's hand covered his lips, hard, and he settled back against the warm chest, waiting until it was safe to whisper.

At last there was no voice in the night except for the regular whisper of the water and leaves and the thumping of two hearts beneath the creek bank. Andy felt the fingers leave his mouth.

"Indians?" he asked, very softly.

"Uh-huh. Four. Headed north."

"You suppose that was the bunch watching the road?" he asked. "Maybe saw everything was quiet and headed back to their camp?"

Ken nodded. Andy could feel the nod, through his head. "Got to be. They went north. I go south."

Andy felt his skin squinch up into goose-pimples. "You can't. There may be more of 'em down that way. They'll get you." He struggled to keep the terror out of his voice.

For once, Ken couldn't rely on shrugs and facial expressions. He had to talk to his brother, there in their dark cranny.

"There's Indians all over the range," he said. "I know they're in the hills to the north. They're after Cobb, that's certain, but who ever heard of Indians that cared which white man they killed? Dry Wells isn't that far away. We've got kin there, people who were friends to our folks. We got to help. To warn 'em. I'm goin'."

"But there's not that many people there. Not enough to fight Indians!"

"There's the telegraph. You know there's soldiers up at the railhead. I heard Cobb say so, and you did too. They stationed 'em there when the hands made so much trouble after the drives last year. No, I got to go, right now. And you got to start here. You know you can't walk that far with your leg the way it is."

Andy felt his stomach turn sick. No, he couldn't walk very far at all, any time. They couldn't get horses. Not without rousing somebody on the place and getting taken back to Cobb. Or without having Quita forbid them to move, which was just about as certain.

Tears leaked from the corners of his eyes, and he was glad of the darkness. "All right. I'll stay low and keep hid good. You...go warn 'em. Say hello to Minta. And her goat."

Ken moved away from him. Andy could hear his feet splash into the creek, heading downstream. That was probably best. The creek wandered toward Dry Wells pretty straight, except for its meandering, until it looped away west a couple of miles north of town.

Andy lay flat, ignoring the pebbles. He tried to stay with Ken as he stumbled along the uneven creek bed. He would get out of it pretty soon, he was sure. Cattle and wild animals traveled along the stream, and there were fair paths to follow. As long as he could hear the water, he was sure not to get too far off course. And the line of trees was a good guideline, too.

It wasn't going to be easy. Ken couldn't possibly make it before daylight. It would probably be nearer noon before he got near enough to find somebody with a horse he could borrow. Someone who'd believe a boy in the middle of the night, bringing word of Comanche attacks in a country where that hadn't happened for a long time.

Andy turned on his side. Minta, now, wouldn't hesitate. She'd get right onto it. Make the mayor get the telegraph operator out of bed, if Ken got there early, and send out the word.

He almost forgot the stones beneath him. He was visualizing the troops being rousted out of their barracks and ordered off into the rangeland. He had listened greedily to tales told by hands who had been in the Great War or in the cavalry or infantry afterward. Some had been in the Indian Wars for a while, until they decided they were getting too old or too attached to their scalps to keep on with soldiering.

So before Ken had gone five miles on his way, his small brother had the cavalry riding to his relief, guidons fluttering in the night wind, bugles sounding, saddles creaking. Officers with sabers. Maybe even Buffalo Soldiers, their dark faces invisible in the night.

All mingled before his inner vision. The pounding of the gallop, the thrill of approaching rescue...all was lost in sudden sleep.

CHAPTER TWENTY-SEVEN

Periodically, Hiram Tolliver sent a couple of his hands to check on his cattle. They worked their way around the range on his ranch, finding small groups here and there and pushing them together toward the bigger grasslands north of the ranch house.

Sim Fraser and his chum Lunt had been working their way around the place for a couple of days, and Sim's disposition was wearing thin. He was a man who liked his creature comforts. A mattress under his bones at night was a thing he prized highly, and grub that was decently cooked was even more valuable to him. His own cooking was terrible and Lunt's was worse, so his stomach was grumbling at him when he rose out of the clump of scrub-oak where the two of them had camped for the night. He wanted to go back to the bunkhouse. He wanted Sara's cooking. But he knew there were cattle over this way—he'd seen day-old droppings and fresh tracks that seemed headed east. So he had to go east after them, and he cursed all the way.

About noon, he heard a shrill whistle from Lunt, who had looped off from his own route, looking for tracks. Sighing, Sim eased his skinny frame in the saddle and heeled Old Red toward the sound. Even when this batch was found, there were still a large number of unfound beasts scattered over Tolliver's ranch.

But what Lunt had located was the scene of another rustling. The ground along the lower parts of a small valley was chopped by double-edged hooves. Running ones, headed east.

Sim joined Lunt on the ground and hunkered down, trying to decipher the jigsaw of hoof marks in the dirt. He thought he caught a glimpse of a horse track amid the mess, and he moved out in a spiral, going wider and wider to find some indication that riders had been hustling the cattle.

When he found a mark, it was of an unshod hoof. Indians? There hadn't been any Indians around Dry Wells for five years that he knew about. No, if Jebediah Cobb could mislead all his neighbors into thinking rustlers were at work among the herds, then there was no reason why he shouldn't try making them think Indians were stealing them, too.

"Come on," he said to Lunt. "We've got to get back and tell the boss about this. He's going to be hoppin' mad when he finds out some more of his animals are gone."

They urged their mounts directly toward the ranch, being able to cut across the range they had so painstakingly zigzagged over before. Even then, it was nightfall before they arrived within sight of the lamp-lit windows.

Sim was hailing Tolliver before Lunt had the horses led away to the corral. "Boss! Hey, Boss! Cobb's been at it again! We got maybe fifteen-twenty head that's been drove off east, out of Mulebone Valley. I knowed that Evans fellow wasn't goin' to help out any. I'd of hung him, if it'd been me!"

The door was blocked by Tolliver's stocky shape. "Sim? What's that you say? Come on in here and tell me."

Sara turned away from the table, which she was clearing of dishes from the evening meal. "Here, Sim. You drink some coffee and have a piece of pie while you talk. You look tuckered out." She whisked a generous slice of pie onto a dish and had him sitting at the table before he knew what was happening.

Tolliver stood by the window. In the lamplight, his square face was turning red, and Sim gulped a bit of coffee before beginning his tale.

"There's a whole bunch of animals been herded out of Mulebone Valley, off to the east," he began. "I cast around till I found a hoof print of a horse. Wasn't shod."

That got all the attention he could have hoped for.

"Not shod? You don't mean to sit there and tell me there's Injuns raidin' my cattle? Man, that's just plain ridic'lous." His face was now a dangerous hue, and Sara pushed her big husband toward his rocking chair and made him sit.

"You just calm down, Hiram," she said. "Here, drink some cool water and breathe deep. There."

Tolliver's color returned to something like his normal high

flush, while his wife fussed over him. He stared at Sim, how-ever, with fire in his eyes. "There ain't been Injuns around here, except for a few Comanch' that go through to hunt, for years. And no Injuns are goin' to raid my land. Nossir, that's got to be that bastard Cobb's work."

Sim nodded, his mouth full of pie. "That's what I think, just exact," he said, around a bite. "And if they're rustlin' east, it's pretty sure they're doin' it to the north and south of the place. No tellin' how many head we've lost without knowin' it."

Lunt came stumping in at the back door, shaking the dust from his clothing. Sara hurried to pour another cup of coffee and dish up another piece of pie.

"What do you think, Lunt?" asked Tolliver. "You think it's our neighbors to the east?"

He nodded, mouth full of pie. He gulped it down and said, "If it was me, I'd get all the boys together and go over to Three Oaks and check out everything on their range. A burnt brand can be spotted easy as fallin' off a horse. With calves, there's no way to tell which ones they stole, but this last batch was full-growed animals. I'd go after 'em. And while I was at it, I'd hang me that rustler we caught before."

Tolliver nodded agreement to every point Lunt made. Sim could tell the boss was really angry—his flare-ups of temper usually cooled down fast enough. But Sim had seen a few real storms in his time and this one looked like it would be a hum-dinger.

Sara, standing in the background as she usually did, now came forward and put her hand on Hiram's shoulder. "You just cool down. Can't go riding off right now, anyway. The hands are scattered all over the place, hunting strays. It'll take a couple of days just to get 'em all in one place and rested up and ready to go. By then, maybe we'll find out what really happened." She glared at Sim, who avoided her glance and tucked into another slice of pie.

She was, of course, completely correct. As usual. It took two days of hard riding on the parts of Sim and Lunt and Hi just to get to the different groups of men out on the range. It took the dribs and drabs of men another two days to get back to the ranch. Fresh horses had to be rounded up from the pastures along the creek, guns and equipment had to be checked, so that it was three days before the little army took off for Three Oaks Ranch.

Tolliver might have a hot temper, but he was no fool. He didn't head directly for the ranch house, which was south and east of his own place. He crossed the creek and went into the hills north of Cobb's land, moving down through the country formerly occupied by his lost neighbor.

Luck or Providence seemed to be with the fifteen men. They didn't see a soul. Not one of Cobb's riders, which was what they expected to find, and not one of Buffalo Hump's warriors, which would have surprised them totally. Perhaps fatally, as well.

Sim, riding point, was no tracker if the truth be known. If he had been looking for Indian sign and had known what to look for, he might have seen faint traces of moccasins and unshod horses. He didn't, and Tolliver, coming behind with a full head of steam, didn't look either. They rode right across the sign telling of Buffalo Hump's movements without even knowing anything was there.

At last, loaded for bear, the group swung slightly westward again and found the cover of the creek. They clattered along the stony bed, their mounts splashing the shallow waters and stopping now and then to drink. The men didn't talk, but they made enough noise to wake the dead, if any had been about.

But nobody, dead or alive, happened to be watching that creek on that day. Buffalo Hump had other things on his mind, having received his vision and made his decision.

Jebediah Cobb, too, had other things on his mind, and his men, leaderless for the moment, were slacking off at everything.

Only José, bedridden now, had an intuition that something was on the way. Something dangerous. But who listens to the ravings of a sick man?

CHAPTER TWENTY-EIGHT

Minta Granger had a sense of humor, along with a temper. That was why she hadn't killed Winthrop many times over. But on this particular morning she was almost at the end of her rope. He had begun the day by eating all her geraniums out of the window boxes she'd built onto the store.

That had been bad enough—it had taken her five years to find someone who would part with cuttings and another two to get the things to the point of blooming. They had been glorious, bursts of scarlet bloom livening up the window-ledges under the porch. Now they were making more goat, inside Winthrop.

After that, chastened after the talking-to she had given him, he had gone sulking out into the back yard and eaten her best night-dress, which had been hanging on the clothesline. She hadn't found that out until she went to take in her wash. The shreds of cotton still clinging to the clothespins weren't large enough to make dust cloths.

It was starting out to be one of those days, she knew, and she tried her best to keep her temper and avoid snapping at her customers. It was with no pleasure at all that she saw Cobb's huge horse plod up to the hitch-rail and the man himself dismount. Jebediah Cobb was not one she could stomach with ease at the best of times.

She drew a deep breath and straightened her shoulders. "Good morning," she managed to say, as he lumbered into the store.

"Ah. Miss Granger. I have ridden in to check on the well-being of my nephews. I have been so very concerned about them...nothing else could have brought me to the point of letting them leave their home."

His words and intonations were entirely false. She knew the way he talked habitually, and this wasn't it. Besides, she hadn't seen her cousins in months.

"And how should I know how my cousins are? I haven't seen them in a long, long time. What on earth has you so concerned about them, anyway?" She listened for his answer with skeptical ears.

"Why...they are showing signs of insanity!" He lapsed into his normal manner of speech. "They've been actin' crazy as a couple of coots. I sent 'em in with Robert Evans a couple of days ago. He was bringin' 'em to the doctor."

Minta turned pale. "A couple of days ago? We haven't seen hide nor hair of them. Not here in Dry Wells. Cobb, you idiot, you've sent those children off with a killer, and he's done away with them. I know it...knew it all along. Don't think you're going to fool me. I've known for years that you were going to try something of the sort."

In his own turn, Cobb turned pale. While he knew that she was absolutely correct in her assessment of his intentions, he also knew that in this case he was quite innocent. And he was wondering desperately what had happened to Evans and the boys. Did the Indians, even now, have them in their hands?

"I sent 'em to Doc Duncan. I swear that's what I did. Just because they acted so crazy, and the Injuns were makin' a problem...." His voice trailed off.

"Indians? What Indians? Cobb, you're not making sense. There haven't been hostiles here in ages." Minta put her hands on her hips and glared at him.

"Comanche," he mumbled. "The ones that used to come through Three Oaks on their hunts. We...had a mite of trouble with 'em a couple of years ago. They got riled at us. Seems the old chief's come back to get even. They got Quita a few days back."

"Got Quita?" Minta was almost choked with rage. "And you're standing here telling me about it instead of being out there looking for her?"

"Oh, Evans and her pa got her back," he said in a placating tone. "Not hardly hurt at all. She's gone back to work just fine, though old José is in pretty bad shape. He's been sick forever, though. It's just finally caught up with him."

Without answering him, Minta moved onto the porch of the store and caught up an iron rod that lay along the window ledge. She swung it hard against a buzzard-wing plow that hung from a chain fastened to the roof. The sonorous clang echoed down the dusty street. Four times she struck the metal, and four gonging summonses brought distant figures onto porches.

Long stepped out onto the porch of the mayor's office and stared toward her. She gestured for him to come. The doctor, farther down, saw her and started, hatless, toward the store.

"Now don't go and get everybody all riled up," said Cobb. He was now sweating profusely. "I feel sure everything's going to be all right. Unless...unless those Comanch' got 'em." The mayor and the doctor had come within hearing range, and the word Comanche stopped them in their tracks.

"What about Comanche? Whatinell have you been doing now?" yelled Long. "I thought you'd torn it for all of us a couple of years ago when you murdered those hunters. You been stirring them up again?"

Cobb stepped off the porch and leaned casually against his horse. "Now, Bob, don't get all upset. Everything's going to turn out all right. We've just got a little problem, right now...." He stepped backward as Long mounted the porch steps and looked him in the eye. Long might be a little man, pretty dried up with age, but he could glare down a sidewinder.

"What sort of problem do you have?" he asked Cobb. There was no room for evasion in his tone.

Duncan, standing on the ground beside the porch, said nothing, but the expression on his long Scottish face told Cobb he'd better tell all the truth at once, or he was in for it.

"Well...old Buffler Hump's back. He didn't die, after all. And he's got his sons and his kin-folks and a bunch of red-skinned troublemakers with him, I think. He got one of my men, the other day. You 'member Ray?"

Minta snorted delicately. She did indeed remember Ray.

"They caught Quita on her way to town a few days ago. But her pa and my new hand got her back right quick before they hurt her any. And now Robert hasn't got here with the boys, though I sent 'em off two days ago to stay with you,

Doc," he nodded down at Duncan, "so's you could see what in tunket's wrong with 'em. Both those kids are actin' really strange."

"They didn't arrive," said the doctor. "And I can't see that either of them could possibly go mad. 'Tisn't in their blood."

"You wouldn't say that if you could see 'em. Droolin' and jerkin' and makin' crazy noises. It's enough to make anybody doubt his own mind. No, if you could see 'em you'd know I'm right. But they didn't come. They're someplace out there...." He gazed across the flatlands toward the north.

"And the Comanche have them, as surely as I stand here," said the mayor. "We've got to get some men together and start a search. You see to that, Doc. I'll go to the telegraph office and send word to Lawson. There's a detachment of cavalry there, and I feel as if I can get some action out of them. They don't like having Comanche roaming around in their territory."

"I'll just go back to the ranch and see if they've maybe made it back home," offered Cobb, his voice hopeful.

"No, you will not. You are going to stay right here in Dry Wells until I am satisfied that you haven't done a thing...untoward...to those children," said the doctor. The mayor nodded, and Minta's eyes glinted with determination.

"You can stay here with me," she said. "There's a rocker back in the back of the store. You sit there, and if you show any signs of bolting, I'll...I'll sic Winthrop on you."

Cobb nodded meekly and went into the store, leaving her to stare glumly at the two men.

"Will we find them alive?" she asked, though she knew that any reply would be purest guesswork.

"There's a chance. A good chance," said Long, turning to head back toward the telegraph office, which was in the side of his own office building.

The doctor stared after him for a moment. "I'd better get a move on, mysel'," he said. "I wish I had the optimism of yon man, though. I canna but think those wee bairns may be gone to join their kin."

Minta shook her head vigorously. "Let's hope not," she said. "And aside from their predicament, do you realize that we are sitting here with not more than a dozen able-bodied men within calling distance, the cavalry a half-day's ride away, and a lot of angry Comanche buzzing around the countryside? There are more people in danger than my cousins, I suspect."

She watched the doctor lope away, his loose-limbed body eating up the ground much faster than it appeared to. She was making plans, true, but she was also thinking of the two boys she had known all their lives. What was happening to them, out there in the wild country?

She shivered and turned back into the store, and the rising breeze flapped the torn WANTED poster dismally behind her.

CHAPTER TWENTY-NINE

Kenneth, like most of his fellow ranchers, wasn't much of a walker. He rode like a part of any horse. He ran, sometimes, with the speed of a jackrabbit, but he had never worked to acquire the endurance needed to walk twelve miles without feeling the effects of it.

Besides which his boots were made for riding. The high heels dug into the dry soil, the pointed toes began to hurt his feet very quickly, and the uppers chafed his calves as he trudged along, keeping the creek on his right and his gaze fixed on a bright cluster of stars.

He knew that it was getting on toward daylight. The feel of the light wind had changed. The smell of the night had altered. The birds that called along the band of trees lining the creek had gone silent. In the distance, there came a long howl, a coyote bidding goodbye to the night hours.

He had fallen into a rhythm of sorts, keeping his breathing paced to his swinging feet. The stars shifted westward, and he picked another clump, smaller and dimmer, to keep him on course. A line of light touched the horizon, making the scrubby oaks and mesquites stand out in stark silhouettes against the sky. It was going to be hot as Hades pretty soon, he knew, and he was still miles from Dry Wells.

If he had only seen those Indians earlier, while he had most of the night to walk, it would have been much better. Now he knew that he would stand out on the rolling countryside to any of the bunch who came back to keep watch.

He cut back into the shelter of the trees along the creek. He slowed, too, for any Indians left on watch might well be stationed along the stream, melting into the shadowy shapes of

124

hunchbacked oaks and cottonwoods and sycamores. He would be hard to see, even if you knew he was there.

Ken devoutly hoped he wasn't there at all.

The sun rose, rolling up the east like a tremendously swollen red ball. The rain from the storm had evaporated long since in the devastating heat, and now the air was full of dust. Ken's steps, even in the shade of the trees, kicked up a thin haze of dust, too, and his nose began to itch.

He kept the sun on his left, and all too soon the creek curved away westward. Now he had to leave its comforting cover and head across the rolling country toward the town.

Something made him drop to his knees behind a mesquite. Some instinct left over from his distant ancestors told him that a watcher was abroad, and he crouched under cover, staring around him in a deliberate circle. The boy's eyes were keen. He spotted the shape of a horse and rider, coming across a ridge to the west. Beyond the creek, so maybe they hadn't spotted him before he went down.

He flattened himself against the prickly earth beneath the mesquite. A line of ants marched beneath his nose, and he wriggled backward a bit. He kept staring through the feathery growth toward the creek. The rider was now invisible behind the tree line, but Ken didn't dare to move away from his shelter.

Now what could he do? He knew that if he rose and walked on toward Dry Wells, it was more than likely he would be captured again by the Comanche. Or shot, which was even more probable.

He looked at the sky, the line of the creek, the curve of the next roll of land. He was still something like three miles from the town. Could he possibly run, stooping, for long enough to clear that swell of land? It was worth trying.

He got to his knees on the farther side of the mesquite. Bending low, he moved toward the ridge, trying his best to stay behind rocks or bushes. A dry wash cut across his way, and he jumped down into it and followed its shallow trench at an angle up the slope.

There came a rustling beside his foot as it came down alongside a sizeable stone. Before he could move he heard the dry chatter of a rattlesnake.

Ken froze in his tracks, his breath congealed in his throat, his heart thudding heavily. He could see from the corner of his eye a dusty slither of coils quivering in the pebbly trench. Sweat, which had been rolling freely down his back and arms, seemed to turn frosty on his skin.

The triangular head swayed, the tongue flickering daintily. Ken breathed very carefully, motionless, trying to still the sound of his blood in his veins.

And then a huge sneeze caught him off guard. Even as he shook with its force, the head darted forward and he felt the sting of fangs in his leg.

"Damnit!" The boy sat on the boulder, for the snake was winding away among the rubble of the wash.

He pulled his pants leg up and dug into his pocket for his penknife. A double thrust, crossing each fang mark, brought blood gushing. He encouraged the flow by squeezing the wounds, but already he could feel the sting of the venom along his veins.

"Damnit, damnit!"

He tore a strip off the tail of his shirt and tied it tightly, feeling the pressure of the blood well up against the ligature. He could see the leg swelling already, an angry flush beneath the skin beginning to bulge outward.

He jerked down the pants leg. Now he had to move, no matter what the Comanche in the trees might think or do. If he didn't get to Dry Wells and Doctor Duncan, he would probably die out there in the sun, raving and rolling in agony.

He sighed deeply, feeling fever begin to build inside him. Then on hands and knees, Kenneth began to crawl toward his destination.

CHAPTER THIRTY

Bao was not the happy-go-lucky fellow he appeared to be. Having sized up the whites among whom he had been forced to live and work for most of his forty years, he played out the role they expected from him flawlessly, but his heart wasn't nearly as enigmatic as he had trained his face to seem.

He had come to work for the owners of Three Oaks before either of their sons was born. They had been hard-working people, kind enough to let others go their own ways without interference. His years with them had been happy enough, and he had felt real grief when they had died in that freakish storm.

Letitia had been another sort entirely. She was, to begin with, an old maid who had never lived a rural life. She was frightened of all too many things, and she had done her best to frighten her nephews as well. Bao had been happy when she married Cobb. The boys needed a man to shape their characters, which stood a good chance of being weakened by their hysterical aunt.

It hadn't taken him long to realize that her marriage was the worst possible move for her, for the boys, and for his own comfort. Cobb, he was certain, had had a hand in the fatal buggy accident that had taken his wife's life. He was even more certain that the children were endangered every day they lived under the man's roof.

Yet what could the Chinese cook do to help them? Cobb objected to his presence and made Quita his personal cook, so Bao was no longer, able to come and go freely about the big house. The boys, however, came to him often, begging him for tales of his native land (which now had grown rather dim in his memory, if the truth be known).

He had been able to keep a shrewd eye on matters in the household, and when Evans arrived he had been apprehensive for a time. And then he had realized that the young man was not what Cobb had thought he was getting. Bao trusted his own assessments of people. He trusted Evans almost at once.

Now, washing dishes after supper in the cookhouse, he was thinking hard about the predicament of everyone on the ranch. The boys were safe, for the time being. Their hiding place was a good one, for even Quita had never been able to find it.

Evans and José were badly at risk if the Comanche made a full-out attack. The small house was at a distance from the ranch house, screened by a stand of trees from view of the larger dwelling and by the big house itself from the bunkhouse and corrals.

It had been proven twice over that it wasn't safe to try getting to Dry Wells by way of the road or the range to southward. Even if all the hands tried to go together, he suspected that they would be picked off on the way. And nobody must know that Evans was here or that the boys had returned...it made a big problem.

Bao finished up, rinsed the dishpan and turned it over to dry. Then he retired to his small room at the back of the cookhouse and picked up his worn copy of the works of Shakespeare. It had been a gift from a long-dead employer, and he treasured it...those plays and verses had given him more than a little understanding of the people among whom he lived.

He read for an hour by the mellow light of his lamp. When he slept at last, he rested uneasily, the problems with which he wrestled squirreling in his mind and chasing away deep slumber.

He woke much later, when there came a tap at his window. "Who?" he asked groggily, pulling on his shabby dressing gown.

"Robert Evans," came the reply. "Hurry, Bao!"

He unbolted his private door to the outside and peered out into the night. He had not lighted his lamp, so he could see dimly as Evans staggered into the room and pushed the door shut behind him.

Now Bao was alert. "What has happened?" he asked in a

harsh whisper. "José? Is he...?"

"No. No, José's hanging in there. It's Andy. He just came in from his hiding place. He got worried, there by himself, because Ken has taken off for Dry Wells, walking in the dark."

Bao sat suddenly on the edge or his narrow cot.

"Why?" he gasped.

"They saw a bunch of Indians heading north. Andy thinks it was maybe about eleven o'clock or so. Ken decided it was a good chance to head out south to warn the folks in town, while the Indians were back in their camp or wherever they were going.

"It wasn't that bad an idea, really, but Andy kept thinking about all the things that could happen to his brother. It's a long way on foot, without the right boots to walk in. And there just might have been more lookouts posted down along the creek.

"Finally, he just had to come in and wake Quita and me and see what we thought. I think he has a pretty good reason to be worried. What about you?"

Bao sighed. "I have worry all night. Not sleep well. Now more worry. And we have no one to send. I cannot go. If I am not here to make breakfast for the hands, there will be questions asked that we don't want to answer. Quita must not go. She already have all the danger she need. José certainly cannot go. And you are not able, either."

Robert shook his head. "I made it this far," he said.

Bao lit his lamp and surveyed the man carefully. "You bleed all over," he said. "Look. There and there and there." He pointed at the bandages, which were showing lines of red where the scraped skin beneath them had cracked open with Evans's movements.

"You go off on horse, you will bleed more. I think you may die if you go."

Robert looked grim. "I'm a lot tougher than you think, Bao. And I'm the only one who can go. Even if we wanted to let Cobb know about this, I couldn't. He didn't come back from Dry Wells, Quita says. Which may mean that the Comanche have him, too."

"You let me put on salve. Redo bandage. Maybe that will help," the cook said, rummaging in his small cupboard for his medical supplies.

"You just tie me together good enough to last until I find Kenneth, and I'll be satisfied," Evans agreed.

When he moved stiffly from the cookhouse, just before first light, he was bandaged as thoroughly as any Egyptian mummy. He hoped he'd last just a fraction as long.

CHAPTER THIRTY-ONE

Buffalo Hump had sat on a low hill all day. He had tried all the ways he knew for bringing a vision, but nothing had worked. He had not the time to fast for three days, which made visions far easier to come by. Every moment his mind was distracted by thoughts of his people.

He knew those others who had come on the war trail with him. They had no personal vengeance to carry out...he knew that they had come for less serious reasons than that. He also knew that Three-Coyotes was a reckless man who tended to lead others into trouble when left to himself too long.

With a sigh, he came down the hill, leading his horse, and stood in the twilight, gazing across the untidy growth of scrub that cloaked the hills. This journey was not going well. This war trail had taken a strange turn, and it left him with a feeling of impending danger.

He mounted his horse and headed toward the big camp. Long before he reached it he could hear cattle snuffling and stamping. Occasionally there came the bawl of a calf or the anxious mooing of a cow. He dug his heels into the horse's flanks.

He had told the men to hunt. What on earth had they done?

He arrived to find a scene of feasting. Chunks of raw beef waited to be spitted over the fire, and Three-Coyotes was red to the elbows with the blood of his kill.

"And what have you done, my brothers, to bring back so many animals to our camp? Cannot the white man follow a trail as broad as this one must be?" he asked, the guttural Comanche words seeming to echo among the stunted trees.

Three-Coyotes swaggered toward him. "We hid the trail well," he said. "And it is well known that the whites are like blind old women when they try to track anything. You told us to hunt, and now we have food for as long as we need." He stared up at Buffalo Hump.

"And did the chief have a useful vision?" he asked, his tone derisive.

"That is none of your concern," said Buffalo Hump. "My sons, come with me. We will make talk, while these young men eat their fill."

His words, as well as his tone, were subtly insulting, but he no longer cared. These others were proving to be of more worry than worth. His sons and his nephews were strong and responsible men. Three-Coyotes and his companions were idlers, big talkers who seldom achieved anything worth noting.

With all his kin, he could count nine warriors. The others, all eleven of them, were undependable, he now began to realize. And his enemy, Cobb, was still alive and unharmed, though he felt certain that the discovery of his man's body had shaken the rancher to his heart.

Now he led the way to the spot where he had made his sleeping place. His people squatted about him as he sat on his blanket.

"We must do what we came to do soon. There arc Buffalo Soldiers at the town where the metal road runs, and it will not be long before someone knows we are here and sends for them. We have watched Cobb's lands and his men. They are wicked people, most of them, sharp and brittle. They will break easily, I think. We must attack them and find Cobb and take him away.

"We will entertain him for a long time before we allow him to die. The others who were there...we will kill them and let them be. It is Cobb who betrayed us and broke the word of his kinsman."

He started around the circle of dark faces, unreadable in the night. But each head in turn nodded.

Hawk Feather, his oldest son, grunted. He was toughened by many years of war and raiding. His voice was seldom heard, but when he spoke it was to the point, and his father always listened to him. "We are few. There are four hands of men on the ranch, and it will be a bad thing to attack them openly. We must pick them off, one by one, as long as they can be caught in that way. We will risk little and gain much. It can be done tomorrow, for they are still going out to their cattle."

Sun-Sets-Red, just younger than his brother, nodded too. "And when we do attack them, there is a way in which we can be certain that our brothers from the tribe will stand with us."

Buffalo Hump leaned forward, interested. "Tell us."

"There are four hands and one finger of them, four hands less one finger of us. Each of us can ride beside one of them, letting Three-Coyotes and Raven's-Beak ride with the chief. It will seem an honor for them. But the chief will be able to keep them under his eye, so that they cannot lead their companions astray."

Buffalo Hump considered. It seemed a good plan, though it was not usually the way of his warriors to attend to anyone except themselves when they went to war. He knew, however, that Three-Coyotes was a very brave man when it came to raiding fields full of women or herds of horses and cattle. He was not very fond of risking his skin against other armed men.

"You do not object to his plan?" he asked his kinsmen, staring about at the shadowy figures.

One by one, they grunted, "No," and he relaxed on his blanket. He had not been given a vision, but he had been given wise and strong sons and nephews. They had devised a good plan, he thought.

"Then tomorrow we will go ourselves, letting these others lie in camp and eat meat, and we will pick off all the men we can. If this goes well, we can attack the ranch at dawn on the day after that. It is good?"

"It is good," came the reply. Buffalo Hump still felt something strange sitting beside his heart but he contented himself with what he had. "Then so will it be," he said.

The others returned to the fire to share the meat, but Buffalo Hump did not. He took some jerky from his pouch and chewed it, ignoring the pain in his teeth that had grown worse with the years.

He wanted none of the white men's cattle. He wanted the white men's blood.

Chapter Thirty-Two

Palmer had never intended to get in so deep. When he'd come to ride for Cobb, before the man's wife died, he was on the run, and he'd thought Three Oaks would be a good place to lose himself for a year or two. He'd found however, that Jebediah Cobb was a man who held onto anything he thought of as his.

His land. His cattle. His nephews. And even his hired hands. There had been time, by now, for Palmer to catch onto the way in which Cobb got every new hand indebted to him or under his thumb in some other way.

A bunch of the hands were at odds with the law, just as he had been. If anyone left, Palmer knew that word would go out to Cobb's friend the marshal, and that would be that. His own case was no different. In addition, there had been that triple-damned run-in with the Comanche, a couple of years ago. He had a sick feeling in his gut that what had happened to Ray, out there in the open country, had put paid to his part in the killing of those savages two years ago. And if that was what they gave to Ray, he'd be getting even worse, for he had bossed the entire operation.

It made Palmer nervous, having Cobb gone from the ranch. He was used to having the boss right at hand, and particularly now that things were strung so tight, he needed someone to tell him what to do. He'd always needed that, which was why he had been in on that bank job that had sent him running in the first place.

But Cobb had gone into town, and it was up to Palmer to keep the men busy. He had no intention of sending them out far from the ranch-house. Not with the Comanche out there. But he saw no reason why they shouldn't hunt out young stuff that had strayed along the creek, pushing them back into the bulk of the herd.

He sent Stinson out wide to one side and Kilpatrick to the other, telling them to watch as if their lives depended on it. Then he took the dozen or so men he'd brought and began pushing through the brush after the strays.

The crack of a rifle shot brought him out of the tangle in time to see Stinson hit the ground and his horse take off for some place quiet and far away. The way Stinson was hit, Palmer knew he was dead. There was something about the boneless flop that was unmistakable. Even as he opened his mouth to yell for the others to hit for the timber along the creek, a slug zinged past his cheek and went whining away through the brush. He pulled his mount around sharply and plunged into a thick stand of scrub oak.

There came a muffled grunt from beyond the thicket, and he dropped off his horse and snaked forward to see who had been hit. Before he could see the man, he felt wet stickiness on his hand as it pushed down a branch. Blood.

Kennedy lay beyond, his throat a mess of blood, his eyes already glazing. Two men gone already, and he didn't even know where the fire was coming from.

Palmer cupped his hands to his mouth and whistled shrilly. Three times he sent his signal, hoping that the men would split up, keep low, and head for the ranch. Then he found his horse again and led him through the scrub, doing his best to keep from making a disturbance.

He worked his way clear of the scrub and mounted on the fly, staying low over the animal's neck. Two more slugs sang over his head, as he flew over the rolling land toward the ranch. He could hear another set of hooves pounding along behind him...he hoped desperately that they belonged to one of his men.

Now he was getting clear of the cover along the creek, and he could see several galloping shapes spread over the terrain. Hoving...yes, and Callou. Kreutz. The others were too far away to identify. He spurred Stony, urging him on with hands and heels and the gelding fairly flew over the dried grass, past mesquite clumps that seemed to flash by, over outcrops of rock. Behind him, the hooves came on, keeping pace with him.

Palmer gained the ridge of ground that arced around the ranch at a distance of a mile of so. He turned in the saddle to look behind him, and his heart turned over in his chest. The man sitting the paint was a Comanche.

He turned his face toward the ranch, praying that he could outrun his pursuer. Stony was gasping, now. He was a good cutting horse, but he was old. His wind wasn't what it had been. Palmer cursed himself for being sentimental and sticking to the nag when he could have had one of the fiery young beasts from the string.

The horse was straining every nerve, his breath coming in great moans of effort. The clumps of cactus and mesquite and oak were rushing past, but not as fast as they had been. Just as Palmer thought the horse would drop dead of its exhaustion, Stony put a hoof in a hole and fell.

Palmer went over his head and landed on his chest, knocking all the wind out of himself. He hadn't enough presence of mind even to be afraid until he was able to breathe again. Then he had enough fear to occupy every fiber of his being.

Buffalo Hump sat on his big paint, staring down at the man who had led the raid on his hunting party. Palmer knew that the man recognized him, knew him for what he was. He found his heart pounding so hard that he almost couldn't breathe.

He rose, when he was at last able to, his legs shaky under him. The fall had scraped the skin from his face and neck, and he could feel a slow trickle of blood running onto his shirt. The cloth grew sticky, as he stood staring up at the Comanche.

"Palmer," said the Indian, his voice calm and deep, without passion.

"Yes." What use was there to deny it?

"You abused my women. You killed my son."

"Yes."

"And you were told to do this by Cobb. Are you no man of your own? Must you do what other men tell you to do?"

The man's tone was curious, as if he really wanted to know. Palmer remembered that Indians were mostly independent of anything white men would call authority. Even chiefs were more like war leaders or wise men, useful when needed but not the bosses of the tribe.

He sighed, and his chest hurt worse. "Cobb could send me to jail any time he decided I wasn't going to obey his orders. Besides...I didn't see no harm...." his voice trailed away into silence as he stared up at the man whose family had fallen victim to him and Cobb.

"You saw no harm in killing Indians. They are vermin, made to be destroyed so that your kind can take all the land between the Great Waters," said Buffalo Hump, still in that detached voice.

Palmer didn't answer. There was no answer. That was what he had been taught all his life, and he didn't intend to deny it now.

"But before we are exterminated, we will entertain ourselves a bit. I had thought to give you death at once, but there will be time. We have killed half your men today. We have the time." He smiled, and it was not good to see.

He raised his hand, and another horse came pounding up. "Take him," said Buffalo Hump.

Palmer backed away as the younger man approached...and someone behind him hit his head hard. Everything went dark, and he found himself wishing, even as he fell, that he would never wake again.

CHAPTER THIRTY-THREE

Cobb had been trying to ease away from the store for hours, but Minta Granger was keeping a sharp eye on his movements, and he hadn't been able to manage it. He had begun to believe that something was badly amiss...something so serious that nothing he could pull off might be able to fix it.

"Better get back to the ranch," he said at last, finding that less obvious tactics hadn't worked. "I don't like to think of my people being out there, with those Comanche around."

Minta turned from the counter, where she had just counted out change to an elderly widow wearing a bonnet as big as she was.

"I think you had better wait for the mayor and the doctor to get back. They'll want to talk to you about the boys. And other things. You just hold on."

"Now. Miss Minta, I don't think you have any authority to keep me waiting like this," he objected. "I've got to be about my business, and if you don't like it, I can't help that."

He found himself staring down the barrel of a sawed-off shotgun, aimed about the middle of his belly.

"Of course I haven't. But if this should accidentally go off, by golly, you'd stay here forever. And I'd be so upset I'd cry for a week." She grinned at him, and for the first time he saw beyond her prettiness to the strength of her jaw and the steadiness of her eyes. She wasn't a person to tempt very far, he realized. She wanted to pull that trigger!

"Now I'm busy and can't waste the time for holding you at gunpoint. So I want you to sit right there in that chair and put your hands behind the back."

He complied, finding nothing coming to mind that would

get him out of his predicament. She tied his hands not only to each other but also secured them to the back rung of the chair. When he tried the tightness, he almost cut off his circulation completely.

He found himself sitting in a corner of the store, concealed from the front by a stack of boxes. That was good. The fool woman thought she was going to keep him here against his will, and she'd be mightily fooled. He'd get even, too, if it took him a year.

She popped from behind the boxes again, and he made himself look blank. It wouldn't do to let her know he was going to escape. She might blow him away before he had the chance.

She was followed by that damned goat she kept for a pet. She pointed to him and spoke to the critter as if it was a Christian. "Winthrop, you keep an eye on our guest. If he tries anything, you butt the ever-loving hell out of him. And let me know, I'll do the rest."

She turned back to her work, leaving the goat standing there gazing at him, with its beard working up and down as it chewed something. The horizontal irises, a wicked yellow-brown, surveyed him sardonically, as if Winthrop too wished he'd try something.

Cobb shook himself. Nonsense! No goat ever born was able to keep watch over a man. He ignored the creature and returned to testing his bonds, twisting his hands until they felt as if they'd burst with the trapped blood. Winthrop watched disinterestedly, still chewing.

The animal glanced down, saw a torn label on one of the boxes, and lipped it off into its mouth. It chewed some more, its gaze never leaving him.

Cobb glanced around desperately. If he could walk the chair over to the window, he might be able to saw the rope in two on the rough edge of the windowsill. That would be a quiet way to go about it. He moved his feet (with difficulty, since she had tied them together) and braced them, rocking the straight chair a bit. One set of legs moved forward minimally.

It was going to take a long time, but he kept at it. The goat still watched philosophically. He had known it wouldn't know what the crazy bitch was talking about.

He worked himself into a sweat, moving the chair a fraction of an inch at a time toward the window. He paused to rest, once he reached the middle of the six-foot space he had to cover.

At that point, Winthrop stopped chewing, lowered his head, and charged. He hit Cobb in the side, just above the belt, and sent chair and man toppling into another mountain of boxes with a mighty crash. Then he stepped back to survey his handiwork.

"Ba-a-a-a-a!" said Winthrop emphatically. Minta pushed past the goat and stared down at Cobb, who was buried sideways in empty boxes. "I told you not to try anything. Winthrop may be a pest most of the time, but he's the best watchman I ever saw or heard about. Now you relax and wait. It's all you're going to do, believe me."

She caught the leg of the chair and jerked it free of the boxes, bringing her prisoner along with it. She didn't set it up again. She left him lying on his side, the weight of the chair making a crease in his right arm. He could have turned onto his stomach and tried to free himself that way, but Winthrop was still there, yellow gaze fixed on him, waiting for just that move. Cobb lay still and tried nothing else.

It was probably the longest afternoon of his entire life. By the time Long returned with word that the cavalry was coming, Cobb had had the time to think over his sins. The list was a lot longer than he had thought, and for the first time in his life he was a bit nervous about some of them.

CHAPTER THIRTY-FOUR

The sun was high now. Ken felt the fever of the venom adding its power to the fever of the sun. He lay curled in the small shadow of a mesquite, resting from his efforts, listening for any sign that the Indian had seen him moving. Surely the distance was too great by now. But he had no way of knowing where the mounted man had gone. He might have hidden himself in the trees along the creek, but he also might have come on into the grasslands east of the creek. He just had to assume that he hadn't been seen and keep on crawling.

Ken coughed, dust thick in his nostrils. If sidewinders had to breathe nothing but dust, no wonder they were so ill-tempered! He stared out at the ground that shimmered with heat. Every pebble was like a coal of fire; even the dust scorched his hands as he crawled. He wished with all his might that he could stay where he was. That someone would come looking for him and take him to Doctor Duncan on horseback. But he knew that was useless.

He thought of Robert, who had come after him and Andy when almost all his skin had been scraped off him. Anybody else, almost, would have quit. Just simply laid down and died out there from exhaustion and loss of blood. Robert had hung on, and he'd got what he came for. Ken intended to try his best to do the same.

The leg was one huge misery, swollen and dark. He knew the blood needed to circulate in it, but if he loosened the tourniquet the venom would circulate, too. No, he just had to hang in there and keep going. He squinted at the sun. He corrected his direction a bit and crawled out from beneath the mesquite.

Once more he moved over the rough ground, frightening

scorpions and lizards and horny-toads. He thought he had come at least halfway, and that was some comfort. If he'd lasted this far, then surely he could last the rest of the distance to Dry Wells.

The next time he rested, he wondered if he would ever be able to set his weight on his bruised, punctured, bloody hands again. His knees were worn to the bone, the legs of his pants being less than scraps from the friction with the rocky soil. His breath was sobbing in his throat but he held back the tears. That would waste water, and he needed all he had inside him if he was to make it in.

He found a big chunky heap of rocks and wriggled into the thinning line of shadow on its west side. He had to curve his body around to keep it in the shade, and he lay with his ear pressed to the ground, trying to regain some strength with which to go on. It was some time before he realized that the regular thudding he was hearing wasn't his own laboring heart.

He pulled himself up, holding onto the stones, until he could prop his body upright, keeping the swollen leg clear of pressure. Somebody was riding a horse across the grassland. Was it the Indian? Or might it be one of his own kind hunting strays, perhaps, or just traveling across the country?

He found that his vision was blurry. He couldn't decide if that was the snakebite or the sun's fault. He shook his head hard, swiped at his eyes with the backs of his wrists, for he couldn't bear to put any pressure on his abused hands.

When he peered over the top of the rock-pile again, he could see something moving through the heat-haze. It was still distant, but it was going in the direction he wanted to go.

He looked at his hands. He felt the immense bursts of pain in his leg. He knew he would never make it without help.

It was worth the risk. He yelled, surprised at how weak his voice sounded. He took a deep breath and shouted as hard as he could. The distant figure seemed to waver. The horse came to a halt, and the mounted man turned his head toward Ken.

"Help!" the boy yelled. "Hel-l-l-p!"

The horse turned toward the pile of rocks, moving slowly as if the man might fear an ambush. But he was coming. Kenneth sagged against the stone, limp with relief. Even if it was an

142

Indian, what could he do that hurt more than this?"

When the rider came close enough to Ken to see his face, the boy thought he must be delirious. It looked like Robert, though he knew his friend was flat on his back, almost unable to move, in José Meléndez's house.

"Robert?" he croaked, knowing he had to be wrong.

Then he knew he was right...the face was tracked with bandages and the eyes were those of his friend. How in the world had he managed to be right where he was needed at just the right time?

The horse came around the outcrop of stone, and Robert stared down at him. "Looks like you've had some problems," he said.

Evans moved as if to dismount. He winced and grunted.

"If I get down from here, Ken, I'll never make it up again. It took Bao doing all he could to get me where I am now. Can you get up here? I can give you a hand...though it looks as if, between us, we couldn't scare up a set of useful fingers to save our souls.

He reached down, and Ken stuck up his arm, waiting for the agony that would be sure to come when Robert gripped his hand. It came sure enough, but they hung on and Ken found himself astride the horse behind Robert.

"Now we ride," the man said. "It looks as if you need some attention mighty soon. But Ken...." His voice sounded a little choked. "...be thinking about maybe having to lose that leg. It looks bad to me. Mighty bad."

Ken clung awkwardly to Robert's waist, using his wrists to maintain a grip. "I been thinkin' about that," he said. "Don't think I haven't. But I reckon it's better to lose a leg than everything else, don't you?"

Evans's body jerked with a grunt of laughter. "You got it right, boy. I've known men with just one leg that had more spunk and get-up than most with two. It's what's in your head that counts, right?"

Ken leaned his throbbing head against the sweaty shirt and closed his eyes. He had never thought help would really come. He had never thought that Robert could possibly get up and ride, not hurt like he had been.

Two miracles had come about, and it seemed it had been on purpose to save him. Maybe his leg would be saved—but that would be three miracles, and he felt a little doubtful about that. A leg and a life were two separate things, he felt certain. "I can run Three Oaks better right now than Cobb ever could," he said to his friend. "I know what he's been up to. I watch and I understand, even if I don't usually say much. I've kept my mouth shut because of Andy. He's too little and too frail to take much upset."

Robert nodded. Ken could feel the motion through his back and the damp shirt. "I know what they're up to, too. We'll put things straight, now that you're both out of Cobb's hands. He didn't come home last night...I wonder what happened to him?"

"I almost wish...." Ken paused. Then he continued, "I almost wish Buffalo Hump would get him. He deserves it."

"You're feverish," said Robert. "You just rest, and we'll be in Dry Wells before you can say scat." Ken closed his eyes again and let the fever take over. It was by far the easiest thing he'd ever done.

CHAPTER THIRTY-FIVE

Robert felt as if he was going to fall into halves, one on either side of his mount. He'd had the devil of a time getting onto the nag to begin with, even with Bao's help. He hadn't really thought he'd find Ken, though he knew he had to try, and the fact that he had discovered him had helped his feelings. For a while.

They were only a couple of miles from Dry Wells now. The clump of dark shapes that was made up of trees and the few buildings there were visible on the edge of his sight, quivering in the heat-shimmer. He could make it that far. He would make it that far.

The sun was overhead, beginning its slide down to the west, and the heat made his scraped skin itch and burn. Kenneth's body heat, augmented by fever, radiated against his back. He felt that he had fever of his own now, anyway. He was burning up, and every bone he owned was protesting in a different sort of ache or twinge or stab.

The dark blot grew larger, separated into store and trees and churches and houses. Figures came into view...busy ones, moving far more quickly than people usually moved on such a hot day at noon. Horsemen...by God!

Cavalry!

Robert forgot his misery, forgot the state of the boy behind him. He stuck his heels into the horse's flanks, urging him to a trot. He made his stiff hand grip the brim of his hat, swung it high, ignoring the pain in his arm and shoulder.

"Heyyyyyyy!" he yelled.

For a bit they didn't notice him, out there on a roadless expanse half hidden, he knew, by the heat-haze. Then a small shape bounded off the porch of the store and galloped toward them. Robert stared. Then he laughed, no matter how it hurt. By heaven, it was Winthrop!

The goat came with incredible speed, circled the trotting horse, scampered back toward the store, and jumped onto the porch. It disappeared into the doorway. Even at that distance, Robert could hear the clatter of something the animal upset as it entered.

Then Minta was on the porch waving her hands, her apron, picking up the broom and waving that. She was shouting, too, and now the cavalrymen were coming to meet him.

Buffalo Soldiers! He recognized the heavy-boned shapes of the mules they rode, saw the dark faces under the caps. He was filled with relief. There was nobody the Comanche respected more than these black warriors, who had fought them to a standstill more times than a few.

The white officer pulled up and turned, keeping his horse in step with Robert's, at a convenient distance for talking.

"Who are you?" he asked. "And what has happened...to both of you?" Kenneth opened his eyes. Robert could feel him shift his weight and survey the cavalryman. The boy's arms tightened about Robert's waist.

"Ken here has been snake-bit. Sidewinder. Tried the walk to town to warn...about Comanch'." Robert's voice faltered, and he felt himself tilting sideways.

Kenneth tightened his grip some more, holding Evans on the saddle. "Hang tight," he said. Then he turned his attention to the officer.

"This is Robert Evans. He rescued my brother and me from the Comanche. He found me, out there where I'd been bit and couldn't crawl any more. He ought to be in bed right now."

"That's the God's truth," the officer replied, surveying them both, his head tilted and his eyes narrowed. "I'm Lieutenant Burkit. We got word there were hostiles in the area. The word came through late yesterday. We got to Dry Wells an hour ago and have been trying to find someone who has actually seen the Indians. Can you talk to me? You look bad."

Robert, listening with his eyes closed, grinned. "This young'un will talk to you, even if they're cutting off his leg," he muttered.

Now they were approaching the store, where Doctor Duncan was waiting for them. The old man took a good look at the problems he was about to deal with and nodded toward the wagon hitched to the rail.

"Put 'em in that," he said. "I'll take the two o' them to my house and work there. There's more to do than can be attempted here. Burkit, you can come wi' them. I suspect you will be wanting to talk to both. It will help keep their minds off what I shall be doing."

Mayor Long, Burkit, and two of the cavalrymen helped to put the two in the wagon, which was trundled off toward the shady spot marking the doctor's house. The tombstones in the cemetery seemed to wink at Robert as they passed and he, feeling deliriously jocose, nodded as they went by the gate.

"Won't be far to take me," he observed. "And high time, too. I feel like death already."

"Be still, mon," said the doctor. "You dinna want to discourage the boy, now do ye?"

Robert shut his mouth...and clenched his teeth, once they laid hands on him to move him into the house. Kenneth yelped as they bumped his leg on the horse's haunch.

The house was cool and shadowy. The high ceilings made it feel cave-like. The white ceilings and the cream-colored walls looked clean and hospital-like, and Robert found himself relaxing. He was in good hands, he felt certain.

He was put on a high cot in a small side-room. "You tend to Ken," he told the doctor. "He's got the real problem. I'm just sore as hell." Duncan nodded. "I'll be wi' ye directly," he said, turning to go.

Burkit passed him, entering. "You feel like talking to me now?" he asked. His tone said that even if he didn't feel like it, Robert was going to.

"Sure," he said. "It's about time. We've had Comanche moving around to the north for days now, and nobody has said a word about it until now. By the way, you haven't seen a man named Cobb, have you?"

Burkit nodded briskly. "Have him over at the lockup behind the mayor's house. Suspicious behavior is the charge we're holding him on, though he claims to be a big landholder around here."

Robert tried to chuckle and groaned instead. "You want me to tell you just why those Comanche are out for blood?" he asked. "You may hang him, once I'm done."

CHAPTER THIRTY-SIX

Buffalo Hump's men followed the remnant of Palmer's men, as they fled toward Three Oaks Ranch. When he had finished entertaining Palmer, a matter that left little even for the buzzards, the old man joined them in the shelter of the trees along the creek.

There was no hurry, now. Two of those he had most hated had paid for their part in the slaughter of the family. Except for Jebediah Cobb, the rest were minor participants in that ugly massacre, and some hadn't even been there at all.

Buffalo Hump waited for twilight. Then he reconnoitered the ranch, riding quietly around the outlying buildings, avoiding the big house where the remainder of the hands were forted up. The small house where José Meléndez lived stood some distance from the ranch house. There was no light there, but the chief dismounted and stepped silently onto the porch. He knew that someone breathed inside...he could feel the presence of a living person there, and he intended to know if that one posed any threat to his plans.

He passed through the outer room, noting as he went, even in the dimness that a sick person had been there recently. He recognized the rags of a shirt—the man who had come after the boys had been here. The sharp scent of some sort of medicine lingered on the air.

The door into the next room was ajar, and he pushed it wider. The click of a rifle bolt sliding home stopped him there in the doorway. This room was darker than the other, but a trace of light still came through the window from the sky. Buffalo Hump saw a dark face against white sheets. The muzzle of a rifle faced him, though the hands that held it quivered perceptibly with weakness and strain.

"You were not there," he said to the man in the bed. "I would have remembered you. Why were you not there?"

José did not pretend to misunderstand his meaning. The black eyes glinted in the faint light, as Meléndez said, "I was not there because I am a man of honor. I do not hurt *mujeres*, and I do not kill those who expect peace from me. I was not there because I would have stopped those *gringos* if I had been." The dying man sighed deeply and let the rifle drop to the bed. "But if you have come to kill me, *gracias*. I am glad to die."

Buffalo Hump stepped nearer, his moccasined feet silent on the scrubbed planks of the floor. He stared down into José's fearless eyes. This was, he recognized, a man...or the last remnant of one. His words might have been lies but his tone could not.

Yet he worked for the villain Cobb.

The Comanche stood quietly, watching José watching him. The man's sickness reeked in the air of the room. He was rotting inside, and every breath he sent into the air brought forth the smell of death. It would not be long before he breathed the last of them...but it would seem like an eternity to him.

Buffalo Hump had lived long, much of that time with pain. He knew about such things. Nothing he could do to this man could possibly equal the thing his own body was doing to torture him. Perhaps he deserved such suffering. Perhaps he did not.

"It is not my decision," he said at last.

A shadow of disappointment crossed the face on the bed. The antique leather of the skin had gone a sickly gray, and the skin had pulled so tightly across the elegant bones of the skull that it looked polished. Death would, the chief knew, be a kindness. But it was a kindness he was unwilling to offer.

"Where is Cobb?" he asked Meléndez.

José laughed, though the sound ended in a gasping choke. "He left the ranch yesterday. He did not come back. We think you have him. Too bad you do not."

"I want him," said the chief, almost to himself. "He is the one I want most of all. The first was an animal, without the

150

mind of a man. The next was a weakling, who cried out under torture. But Cobb is the one, the evil one, who set them onto my people. I want to remove his skin, a strip at a time, with red-hot knives. I want to cut his eyelids away, so that he cannot refuse to see what I am doing to him."

José closed his own eyes and swallowed painfully. When he opened them again, he said, "He deserves every bit of that and more. He kill his wife; I cannot prove, but I know. He have try to get rid of the children. He have try to get rid of me, but I am too old a wolf to fall into any trap that man can make."

A wave of pain seemed to sweep over the man, and he clenched his teeth against it until it passed. Buffalo Hump could see sweat pop out in beads on his forehead.

"I make my own trap, *no es verdad?*" José tried to laugh, but he groaned instead.

Without another word, the Comanche turned and left the house, breathing deeply of the dusty air to remove the taint of death from his nostrils. He had learned something. Cobb had gone to town and had not returned. This meant that it was possible the pony-soldiers had been summoned. If that was true, then it was going to be much harder to get his hands onto Cobb. The rest of these men didn't matter.

He led his horse toward the creek, where he twittered sleepily, a bird disturbed at his rest. His sons and his nephews appeared magically from the dark covert.

"We will wait here," he said. "If Cobb went to call for the soldiers to help him, then they will return to this place. We must ambush them and take him away to the north."

"Our tribesmen wait for us in the hills," said Hawk Feather. "I will go and bring them here."

"A good plan," said his father. "Tell them we will taste blood before tomorrow is done if the whites do as they usually do." His son rode away into the darkness, and Buffalo Hump loosed his own mount to graze. He sat beside the slow-moving water of the creek, watching the distant pinpoints of light that were the windows of the ranch house.

Tomorrow he would see Cobb again, and tomorrow Cobb would die.

CHAPTER THIRTY-SEVEN

By the time Evans had finished telling Burkit everything he could think of, Doctor Duncan had returned and was doing painful things to him. First he stripped off the caked bandages that Bao had freshened that morning, frowning at the scent of the pungent salve the cook had used.

"What sort of medicament ha' you been puttin' on yoursel'?" the doctor asked, as he sponged the torn skin with alcohol.

"Something Chinese of Bao's," said Robert. "He swore it's been used over there for a thousand years. And I have to say it did help. I'd never have been able to ride without it."

Duncan snorted, his brows meeting over his sharp eyes. "Heathen superstition," he muttered, as he rewound Evans's legs with fresh bandage and turned to work his way up his body.

Robert bit his tongue. When Duncan paused to get more bandage, he managed to ask. "Will I be able to go with the cavalry, Doc? I'd like to be there. See how Quita and Andy are doing. I keep worrying about those two and Bao. No telling what those Comanche are dong while we're fooling around here."

"If you're a fool, you're able to go," said the doctor. "No but a brainless booby would take the chance of reopening these abrasions. However, I suspect ye're just the sort to do such a witless thing. If you can sit a horse, I suspect ye'll do." Duncan secured the last of the mummy-like wrappings and held out a hand to help Evans sit up.

"Damn!"

"Told you, didn't I?"

"I'll still make it. Just give me a minute to get my breath.

Ugh! I feel as if old Buffalo Hump had got his hands on me."
Robert flexed his hands, moved his legs, and contained the
groans elicited by the movements.

"Has Burkit got things ready to move out?" he asked.

Duncan moved to the window and peered out. "Looks like
it. It'll be dark by the time you get out to Three Oaks, ye ken.
Not a healthy time to go about looking for Comanche."

"I'd better get out there and find a horse. Mine is tired out."
Robert sighed and stood on his battered feet.

"You may borrow mine," Duncan offered. "I canna think
why I keep a riding beast...I go where I go in the buggy. Take
him. I'll send Miguel to saddle the animal for ye."

It took ten minutes for Robert to get himself out of the
house and onto the nervous gelding, which seemed not to like
the idea of leaving his snug stable so late in the afternoon. By
the time he was mounted, had reassured himself by questioning
the doctor as to Kenneth's condition, and turned the horse toward the shady spot where Burkit had his troop ready to move
out, Robert was asking himself why in hell he was so determined to go on this expedition.

"I'd like to ride along with you," he said to Burkit.

The lieutenant looked him up and down. A faint hint of a
grin touched his lips. "If you can keep up, keep up. If not, turn
back. I wouldn't like to ride if I stood in your shoes."

"I've seen those Indians. I have an idea where to find the
people I want to save. And I know pretty well who was in on
that ambush that brought all this down on us. I'll keep up." He
kicked the gelding in the flank, and the animal sighed disgust-
edly and moved after the Buffalo Soldiers.

Duncan was right. It was fully dark by the time they came
over the ridge and started down toward the ranch house. Evans
edged up to ride beside Burkit.

"Over there—maybe a half a mile—is where I saw them
with Ray," he said. "It's another three-quarters of a mile to the
house. The creek runs along on the other side, winding around,
pretty well grown up with trees and brush. I'd be careful approaching the ranch. No telling what's been happening since I
left this morning."

Burkit grunted a reply. He was moving his men slowly, and

now he ordered the troop to spread out, taking advantage of the occasional clump of oak or mesquite. Robert, finding himself at the far end of the line, turned aside from the track and urged his mount around a long hummock toward José's small house.

Behind him, he heard the occasional clink of metal, the creak of saddle leather, the faint thud of hooves. It was too dark for anyone to see that he had gone, and that suited him fine. He intended to get Quita and Andy and Bao out of there before any sort of battle could break out.

The strip of trees separating the big house from the Meléndez cottage loomed against the stars, after a bit. Robert slid off his horse, tied the beast to a tree, and moved cautiously toward José's rear window. It was open, of course, as it must be in the heat of summer.

"José!" Robert hissed.

The quality of the silence changed. Someone was there, listening.

"José!"

"*¿Quien es?*" came the reply.

"Evans," he said. With excruciating effort, he boosted himself into the window and found himself standing in the pitch-dark room. "Where are Quita and the boy?"

"The Comanche...he have come here," said José. "I send the young ones to hide after you leave, which is good thing. Buffalo Hump stood inside this room. He look at me for a long time, thinking if he must kill me. Then he say, 'It is not my decision'." The sick man gave a rueful chuckle. "He think nothing he do can hurt me more, so he go. But I worry about Quita and the boy. You find them...you have men with you?"

"The Buffalo Soldiers," said Evans. "Cobb got to Dry Wells and told the mayor that Comanche were up here. Long sent for the cavalry. They were trying to find out what they were up against when Ken and I got to town."

"Kenneth? He is safe, then." José gave a small sigh of relief.

"Well...not quite. He got snake-bit. If I hadn't come along in time, he likely would have died out there between the creek and the road. But I did get there, and the doctor says he will be all right, though that leg may have to come off if infection sets in. He's got a fever, but Miss Minta and the doctor's house-keeper are taking care of him." Robert tried to smile reassuringly.

José's gray face was still, guarded. "Then go and find Andy. When you had gone, I was very afraid. I felt the Comanche coming, though they were very far away. I have known for a long time that the boys know a hiding place where nobody find them. I make him take Quita there."

"Where?" asked Evans. "Maybe I can get to them and be there, if the troops and the Comanche get into a real fight. I'd like to know somebody with a gun was with 'em."

"I do not know. It might be someone make me say, *comprende*? If I do not know I cannot say."

"Well, I sure as hell need to know where to look. The cavalry is riding into the yard right now, I suspect. And the Comanch' are waiting for them. What direction should I go? Have you any idea at all?"

"Toward the creek," whispered José. "Somewhere along the creek. Go silently. Take care. Death is in the trees. I feel him. I wish...that he would visit only me."

Robert reached to take the hard-palmed hand in his. He gave it a squeeze.

"I've known a few real men in my time," he choked. "You're right up there with the best of 'em, *amigo*. Don't worry, I'll see that Quita is taken care of. As long as she needs it."

He released the dry, quivering hand and turned away. He left by the window, seeming to forget, for the time, the pain of moving.

He stopped to listen before approaching the creek. Voices sounded toward the big house. A horse snorted loudly. Then, in the distance he heard the pounding of many hooves. Horses were coming at a gallop. From the north, he thought. He dropped and, once more, crawled on scabbed knees toward the dark line of cottonwoods marking the stream.

CHAPTER THIRTY-EIGHT

Hi Tolliver was furious. His normally quick temper, which faded fast in most cases, had been I fanned to a flame by his last losses. It was bad enough to have outlaws making free with his cattle. To have a neighbor stealing them and at the same time making a fool of him was more than he could tolerate.

Sara had tried to calm him, to get him to take the time to go to see Cobb and find out all he could before riding off armed for bear. Usually, he listened to her. She had a cooler head and better judgment. But this time he was beyond restraint. He armed his men, had them catch and saddle fresh mounts, took enough rations to see them through a short military campaign. He hadn't forgotten how to move out a troop...three years of war had taught him a lot that he'd never forget as long as he lived. They retraced the route to the spot where cattle had been driven into the hills north of Three Oaks grasslands.

"You want we should follow 'em up into the scrub?" asked Sim.

"The herd can wait," said Tolliver. "I want Cobb! I want him right now, between my hands or at .the end of a rope. We go south." They rode easily as the sun set, saving the horses for any demands that might wait for them when they reached their goal. By the time they could see tiny points of light marking the windows of the big house, it was dark.

"Sim, you take Red and Bear-Butt and slide around toward the east. Creek's on the west, so won't mess with that timber in the dark. The rest of us'll ride straight in. If they meet us with fire, then, by damn, we'll give 'em more than they bargained for." Tolliver bent over the neck of his horse and peered toward the house.

156

"Funny. There's not a light in the bunkhouse. Just in the main house. Cook shack is dark, too. Well, it's too late to change plans now. In we go." He spurred his big mount to a gallop, and the rest of his men followed suit. Nine came after him, pounding toward the corrals, skirting the outbuildings and approaching the front yard and fence. Three, with Sim, swung wide and came in from a different angle.

A shot cracked through the dark. Rifle, sounded like Army issue. Tolliver dropped from his horse and sheltered behind the stack of boulders marking the end of the drive. He could hear horses up ahead. Another shot snapped into the night, and he whistled the signal for his men to take cover and pick off anybody they could see.

Glass shattered in one of the windows of the house, and all the lights he could see were now out. Someone shouted an order. Damn, they sounded organized. He hadn't realized that Cobb would have a bunch of ex-military people working for him.

He whistled again. Fall back and take cover again. If they were that alert and ready to fight, then he'd wait 'em out until morning, when he could see what was happening.

He scuttled backward, and his big horse came after him, head down, trying to make out what his rider was doing. When he reached the shrubbery he had noted as he came through, he paused and twittered quietly.

Even through the sharp exchange of gunfire, he could hear answering twitters. Four of his hands joined him in his covert, and they crouched there, trying to figure what was going on. There seemed to be a real battle taking place around Three Oaks Ranch house, and for the life of him, Tolliver couldn't understand who the third party might be.

"You think some other neighbor picked tonight to go after Cobb?" he whispered to the nearest dark shape.

"Doubt it." That was Link, sparing of words, as always. "I think we've got ourselves right in the middle of a private war."

"I think you're right. But now what do we do? We won't know who we're shooting in the dark here." Someone was shouting now, but the guns continued to rattle. It was impossible to make out any words. In a few minutes, the shooting died away.

Into the quiet came a voice. "You are firing on the U.S. Cavalry! Cease firing at once! Cease firing at once!" The sharp spat of a rifle answered him. A mocking voice called, "You think you smart Injuns can fool us? We seen what you done to Ray. We know who shot us up this mornin'. If you think you can take us, come on and try, but don't try to trick us. We don't buy it!"

Tolliver drew a deep breath. "It really was Injuns," he said. "And those idiots in the house think whoever's out there claiming to be cavalry is really Comanche. You s'pose it could really be the military?"

Link hawked and spat on the ground between his boots. "Possible. In which case I don't want to get mixed up in this."

"It wasn't Cobb talking from the house," said another voice. "I worked for the bastard for about five and a half minutes. That don't sound a bit like him. Don't sound like Palmer, either. You reckon the injuns done got both of 'em?"

Tolliver considered that for a bit. "No matter if they did or didn't, I think we'd better pull out of here. We don't want to accidentally get into a shooting war with the cavalry boys. That don't make you a bit popular with the government. And being as we're this close to Dry Wells, I think we ought to ride into town, as if that's where we was going all the time, and swear out a complaint against Jebediah Cobb for cattle stealin'. We can wake up the mayor, if he's already asleep, and get it done all legal and aboveboard."

It wasn't easy to get his men together in the darkness. Sim and his group, in particular, were beyond whistling distance and, knowing that there were probably Indians close by, Tolliver didn't want to attract any attention. They finally moved out, very quietly and cautiously, with seven men and headed toward Dry Wells.

As soon as they were over the ridge, they began to hurry. By the time the morning stars were beginning to peep over the eastern horizon, they were riding into Dry Wells.

"You wait here," Tolliver said to the main group, as they pulled up at the dark and silent store. "Link and I'll see if we can rouse the mayor." The mayor, however, was not at home.

This was a puzzler. Tolliver went around the house, looking for signs of anyone's presence. There were lights down at the doctor's house...somebody must be bad, he thought...but nothing showed any sign of a living human being.

The lockup, a small stone building a few paces from the back door, was likewise dark. Tolliver had never known it to have more than one overnight tenant, usually a drunken hand or a cattle thief lucky enough to be held for the marshal. As he stared at the building he realized that he was hearing a noise from inside. A furtive sound, it consisted of small clinks and rattles. There came, in addition, a scraping sound.

A line of lighter color was touching the east, but no light had reached the land below. The door scraped against the sill again. A man slipped through the narrowest crack possible and when he turned, Tolliver recognized the bulky shape.

"Cobb!" he said, very softly. At the same time he caught the man by the scruff of his neck. "By the Great Horn Spoon, I never thought I'd be so lucky!"

Cobb gasped with shock. His big body seemed to wilt in Tolliver's grip, as the rancher marched him away to the spot where his men waited. They rode away as quietly as they had come. Only Winthrop knew, and Minta was at Duncan's, nursing Kenneth. His warning bleat went unheard.

CHAPTER THIRTY-NINE

Robert was racking his brain. Andy had hinted, many times, that he and his brother had a foolproof hiding place. He had giggled at Evans's teasing attempts to guess where it might be. Ken, of course, had maintained his usual silence, so there was no help there, but Andy had taken great pride in finding a place his uncle had never dreamed existed.

There had been something he should remember. Some consistency? Some hint...some...wait! They had always, now that he thought of it, been riding within sight of the creek. Andy seemed to think about his hidey-hole when he was near the stream.

It was a slender clue, Robert knew, but it was all he could come up with. He crept through the light growth, moving nothing if he could help it, as he slid between bushes and through patches of dried grass. Before he found the water, the gunfire had broken out behind him. A real battle, it sounded like. He wouldn't have thought the Indians would be around the house, somehow, but evidently they had fooled him. He wondered where Cobb's hands were. They were crooks, but he hadn't thought they were cowards.

He froze, curling around the roots of a patch of scrub. A Comanche was standing silently beside a tree, his body almost invisible. Only a slight motion had caught Robert's eye in time to keep him from blundering directly into the watcher.

That didn't sound like the Comanche to him. They all went into battle if there was one at hand. He hugged the bush and waited, trying not to breathe, as the Indian stepped away from the tree and turned back into the thicker growth along the creek. Oh, fine! Not only did he have to search the stream in pitch

160

darkness, he also had to avoid lurking Indians as well!

There came a soft burst of gutturals, at a distance but quite distinct, even against the crackle of gunfire. Someone laughed, a deep, "Ho! Ho!" that sounded genuinely amused. It was the voice of Buffalo Hump, Evans felt certain. He had never heard the man laugh, but somehow he knew he would sound just so. And if Buffalo Hump was here, the rest of his bunch had to be, too. In which case, who was Burkit fighting in the yard of Three Oaks?

Evans sighed. He had never had it easy, that was certain. But since he had taken this job his life had become harder by leaps and bounds. He'd never intended to accept the responsibility for anybody. Now he was saddled with three orphans if he counted Quita, who would soon be one.

Strangely enough, he didn't find the burden galling. Not at all. His father had been right, after all. A man grew up, if he lived long enough, and came to know that if he didn't do something useful, there was no point in his living at all.

He waited, ears straining. There was no other sound, and at last he moved again, snaking along toward the faint sound of water moving against pebbles. Now that he was lying flat, every scrape and bruise and cut on his hide was making itself felt all over again. It became very hard to make his legs move, his abused knees touch the ground. His breath began to come hard, sharp in his throat. Now he was very near the water. He laid his cheek down softly, feeling the ripples lap at his hot skin. He took a sip, then another. The coolness went down comfortingly. He slid forward until he was in the water, moving himself along the rough stony bottom without adding any note to the voice of the stream.

He felt foolish. How on God's green earth could he find two people who were hiding as tight as they could from Indians? In the dark? Without calling out. Ridiculous!

He was going downstream. He knew that the banks were low, upstream, and he figured the lair must be an undercut part, where bushes and water weeds grew up to conceal it. He had to do something. Risk or not, he had to find a way to attract their attention. He took a rounded pebble from the bottom of the stream and pitched it off to his right. It thocked softly into wood. He'd hit a tree. He went still, listening.

Nothing.

He moved a few yards farther and clicked two rocks to-gether, very softly. Hardly as loud as a cricket, the clicks chat-tered. Here the sound of gunfire was almost lost. From the right bank came a click. Just one. A couple of heartbeats later, there came another. He slid over to the right.

"Andy?" His cautious whisper hardly carried past his lips.

A hand came out of nowhere, touched his shoulder, his face, then tugged at him vigorously. He pushed himself through a tangle into a space that felt enclosed. He had been right. It was an undercut, almost at water level, yet sloping upward at the back so as to be dry when the creek rose.

"Quita? Andy?" he said again.

"Robert? How did you find us?"

"Used my head. Thought about what you said, from time to time. Sneaked through Indians and underbrush. There's some-thing going on up at the house. Somebody is fighting somebody else, but all the Indians, I'd bet my boots, are hiding in the trees just watching. And laughing."

"*Mi padre*," said Quita. "He is...all right?"

"As much as he can be. He was the one sent me after you two. We'd best stay here, snug and out of sight, until we can sort out what is going on at Three Oaks."

Andy caught his breath. "Did you find Ken?" he asked.

Robert hated to answer him. The kid would worry, and he couldn't do a thing to help. But he deserved an honest reply. "He got snake-bit," he said.

At least, the tale of his hunt for Ken passed some of the time, there in the black slot in the creek bank.

CHAPTER FORTY

Buffalo Hump had never understood whites, even when he lived among them. The missionary-teachers had seemed not to comprehend the way that human beings were supposed to exist. They had strange ideas about suffering and atonement. Nothing they said made any sense...not to a man who thought.

He had come all the way to this place to avenge family. Now he found himself watching a strange sort of comedy. The whites were killing each other. He did not know if Cobb was one of them, and he hated to think the man might die easily from a bullet, but he was enjoying the entertainment.

He was no fool, was old Buffalo Hump. He hadn't the slightest intention of taking his handful of men into a battle between two forces of unknown size, particularly when Hawk Feather rode in to report the arrival of another sizeable group from the north. Let the white-eyes have it out among them. He would wait. There would be another time to learn about Cobb.

When light touched the east, he took his men away. Not to the north and west, which they had expected, but to the south. He hoped, while these men were sorting out their problems, to find some one who might tell him where his old enemy was. If Cobb was back there at the house, that was that. But if he had taken refuge, as the old chief suspected he might, in a safer place, then that place might prove less safe than he had thought. He left the bulk of his men hidden along the creek and rode over the scrubland toward the small town. He was not officially at war with anyone in Dry Wells, and there might be no overt hostility if he stopped there to make it known that his people had crossed the land on a hunting expedition: they had done that for more years than there had been whites to see.

He had not expected more than a scant word about Cobb, if that. When he saw the group riding out toward the west he was puzzled at first, then curious. Why did white men move so quietly and secretly? Where were they going?

He rode back to his men on the creek, and they all went to follow the horsemen he had spotted. When they got near enough, the old man realized that in their midst rode his old enemy.

Cobb did not look happy. His hands were tied to his saddle...he was a prisoner! What had he done to make these men of his own breed turn against him?

It was too good a chance to miss. Buffalo Hump signaled to his sons and the others to pause while he rode on alone. He held his right hand in the sign of peace as he approached the dusty crew.

The oldest of the men came out to meet him. He looked cautious, which was sensible. "I greet you," said the Indian. "And I ask a question." He was staring at Cobb. Cobb looked up, recognized him, and turned deadly pale. His big body seemed to shrink like a punctured bladder, and he sagged on his horse.

"I greet you," said the old man, his tone noncommittal. "I will answer you if I can."

Lying was an art Buffalo Hump had studied carefully in his dealings with the whites. He had never, however, become comfortable with the art. Now he decided to go his own way, whatever might come of it.

"Two years ago, I traveled here with my family, after hunting. This man...," he nodded toward Cobb. "...set his men on us. They raped and killed my women. They killed my son. They tried to kill me but I lived and went away to heal. I have returned." He spoke calmly, without anger.

"This man?" asked the other. His tone was strange and a light of interest came into his eyes. "You are certain this was the man?"

"This man is Jebediah Cobb. I saw him rape and knife my second wife. I saw him order his men to attack us. Yes, I am certain."

"And you want...?"

"I want him as you would do if you were in my place. "

A wicked grin split the fellow's weathered face. He turned his horse and rode back to face Cobb, staring at him, as Cobb began to shake. "Guilty as sin," he said. "You want him, I reckon you have the better right. He only stole my cattle. If he'd killed my wife it would be a different tale, you'd better believe me."

Tolliver led the horse on which Cobb was sitting. He came near Buffalo Hump and put the reins into his hand. "He's yours. Hiram Tolliver's my name, and I pride myself on reading men. I trust you to do...what is just!'

The old chief raised his head, his eyes bright. "I will deal with him as gently as he would deal with me," he said.

Tolliver laughed aloud. "That's just what I wanted to hear!" He turned back to his men and they rode away in a cloud of dust, leaving Buffalo Hump to lead his subdued prisoner back to his own group. "We ride north," he said. "And when we come again to our own place, we will make this one pay for his crimes." He wondered that the white man had turned one of his own over to a Comanche. But whites were a strange breed. They might do almost anything if they found a reason to.

Epilogue

The affair at Three Oaks Ranch took a long time sort out. The cavalry had acquitted itself well, killing no men, taking cover by the book, and waiting out the darkness until things could be resolved.

The hands in the ranch house had taken two wounded. One had died later despite Doctor Duncan's best efforts. Nobody ever knew that another group had been there to reckon with Cobb, though the muddle of hoof prints had confused every tracker with the Buffalo Soldiers.

Robert brought out Quita and Andy when the sun rose, and sneaked with them to a point from which they could see what was going on around the house. When they checked on José, they found him still hanging on, waiting with dignity for his end to come.

Andy went with Robert and the cavalrymen back to Dry Wells. He was sick with worry about his brother. Quita was content to stay with her father. Bao moved into their house to help, which relieved Robert's mind somewhat.

They arrived in Dry Wells to find the mayor, the doctor, and Minta in confusion. Cobb had disappeared in the night, and they could find no trace of him. No horse was missing. No sign of him could be found anyplace in town.

"It's as if the ground opened and swallowed him up," said Minta. "I cannot imagine what has become of him."

"I hope we never find him," said Andy. "I want Ken to come home and run the ranch and fire all the hands except José and you and Bao."

Lieutenant Burkit stepped onto the porch to join them. "I suspect you may want to keep Evans, here, won't you?"

Andy looked surprised. "Of course. We couldn't do without Robert now."

The lieutenant was staring at the wanted poster on the porch. Robert, feeling slightly sick, followed his gaze.

The picture was gone. Only WANTED in faded letters still flapped in the wind. The face was missing.

"You might as well take that down," said Burkit. "It isn't a bit of good as it is."

Minta grinned at Robert. There was a wicked twinkle in her eyes.

"You're right. It's been there for years...and only now has Winthrop decided it's good to eat. Here!" She ripped the paper from the wood, and it crumbled in her hand as she wadded it. Winthrop came out from behind a barrel and looked up at her, his yellow eyes alert.

"Oh, you might as well, I guess," said Minta Granger. She handed her goat the poster, and the last remaining remnant of Robert's criminal past disappeared into Winthrop's stomach.

"We'd better go see to Ken," said Andy. He ran toward Duncan's house, while Robert walked beside Minta.

He wondered how much she knew and how much was just suspicion. She hummed as she walked.

He suspected that he would never know.

ABOUT THE AUTHOR

The author of sixty-two books, more than forty of them published commercially, **ARDATH MAYHAR** began her career in the early eighties with science fiction novels from Doubleday and TSR. Atheneum published several of her young adult and children's novels. Changing focus, she wrote westerns (as **Frank Cannon**) and mountain man novels (as **John Killdeer**). Four prehistoric Indian books under her own name came out from Berkley. Historical western *High Mountain Winter* was published by Berkley Books under the byline **Frances Hurst**.

Recently she has been working with on-line publishers. *A Road of Stars* was her first original novel to appear in print-on-demand format. Many of her out-of-print titles are now available from e-publishers fictionwise.com and renebooks.com; other OP novels are soon to be reprinted via the Borgo Press imprint of Wildside Press and Amazon.com.

Now in her seventies, Mayhar was widowed in 1999, after forty-one years of marriage, and has four grown sons. The bookshop she ran with her husband for fifteen years was closed after his death. She now works at home, writing short fiction and nonfiction, and doing book doctoring professionally. Her web pages can be found at:

w2.netdot.com/ardathm/
and
http://ofearna.us/books/mayhar.html

www.ingramcontent.com/pod-product-compliance
Lightning Source LLC
Chambersburg PA
CBHW051919240626
47153CB00004B/1284